HARLEQUIN®
~Presents~

What have we got for you in Harlequin Presents books this month? Some of the most gorgeous men you're ever likely to meet!

With *His Royal Love-Child*, Lucy Monroe brings you another installment in her gripping and emotional trilogy, ROYAL BRIDES; Prince Marcello Scorsolini has a problem—his mistress is pregnant! Meanwhile, in Jane Porter's sultry, sexy new story, *The Sheikh's Disobedient Bride*, Tally is being held captive in Sheikh Tair's harem...because he intends to tame her! If it's a Mediterranean tycoon that you're hoping for, Jacqueline Baird has just the guy for you in *The Italian's Blackmailed Mistress*: Max Quintano, ruthless in his pursuit of Sophie, whom he's determined to bed using every means at his disposal! In Sara Craven's *Wife Against Her Will*, Darcy Langton is stunned when she finds herself engaged to businessman Joel Castille— traded as part of a business merger! The glamour continues with *For Revenge...Or Pleasure?*—the latest title in our popular miniseries FOR LOVE OR MONEY, written by Trish Morey, truly is romance on the red carpet! If it's a classic read you're after, try *His Secretary Mistress* by Chantelle Shaw. She pens her first sensual and heartwarming story for the Presents line with a tall, dark and handsome British hero, whose feisty yet vulnerable secretary tries to keep a secret about her private life that he won't appreciate.

Check out www.eHarlequin.com for a list of recent Presents books! Enjoy!

*Legally wed,
but he's never said,
"I love you."
They're...*

**The series where marriages are made
in haste...and love comes later.**

**Look out for more WEDLOCKED!
wedding stories available only from
Harlequin Presents®.**

Sara Craven

WIFE AGAINST HER WILL

HARLEQUIN®

TORONTO • NEW YORK • LONDON
AMSTERDAM • PARIS • SYDNEY • HAMBURG
STOCKHOLM • ATHENS • TOKYO • MILAN • MADRID
PRAGUE • WARSAW • BUDAPEST • AUCKLAND

ISBN 0-373-12544-5

WIFE AGAINST HER WILL

First North American Publication 2006.

Copyright © 2006 by Sara Craven.

This edition published by arrangement with Harlequin Books S.A.

® and TM are trademarks of the publisher. Trademarks indicated with ® are registered in the United States Patent and Trademark Office, the Canadian Trade Marks Office and in other countries.

www.eHarlequin.com

Printed in U.S.A.

All about the author...
Sara Craven

SARA CRAVEN was born in South Devon, and grew up surrounded by books in a house by the sea. After leaving grammar school she worked as a local journalist, covering everything from flower shows to murders. She started writing for Harlequin in 1975. Sara Craven has appeared as a contestant on the U.K. Channel Four game show *Fifteen to One* and in 1997 won the title of Television Mastermind of Great Britain.

Sara shares her Somerset home with a West Highland white terrier called Berlie Wooster, several thousand books, and an amazing video and DVD collection.

When she's not writing, she likes to travel in Europe, particularly Greece and Italy. She loves music, theater, cooking and eating in good restaurants, but reading will always be her greatest passion.

Since the birth of her twin grandchildren in New York City, she has become a regular visitor to the Big Apple.

PROLOGUE

IT WAS raining heavily, but the girl paying off the taxi did not turn up her coat collar, or try to avoid the rivulets of water running across the pavement. She seemed oblivious to the wet chill of the evening, pausing under a street lamp to check the address on the scrap of paper clutched in her hand.

It was just one of a number of similar tall houses in the terrace, its neat front door reached by a short flight of railed steps. There was a polished brass plaque by the entrance, and an equally burnished doorbell beneath it.

She touched the button, but it was damp and her fingers slipped. Or was she beginning to lose her nerve? She took a deep, steadying breath, then pressed the bell again, more firmly.

Her ring was answered promptly by a man in a porter's uniform.

'May I help you, miss?' His tone was civil but guarded.

She said, 'I'd like to speak to one of your members—a Mr Harry Metcalfe.'

His brows lifted, and she found herself being closely scrutinised.

'Mr Metcalfe is attending a private party, miss. I don't think he would wish to be disturbed. But I could take a message, if you like.'

'I'm afraid that won't do.' She lifted her chin. Returned his stare. 'I need to talk to Mr Metcalfe myself. It's—urgent. So will you get him, please?'

For a moment she wondered blankly what she would do if he simply denied her Harry again and shut the door in her face. But, grudgingly, he stood aside, and she walked into a large square hallway panelled in dark wood.

Straight ahead a wide flight of stairs, carpeted in deep crimson, curved away to the upper floors. On her right was a desk, with two telephones, and the club's registration book with a pen tray beside it. There was also a newspaper folded at the crossword and a mug of tea, half-drunk, beside it.

And on the other side of the hall was a series of doors, all closed.

Behind one of them, she supposed, was Harry, centre of attention at his private party. But which one?

The porter opened the nearest door, motioning her to precede him into the room beyond. He pressed a switch, bringing two heavily shaded wall lights into service.

'If you'll wait here in the reading room, miss, I'll see what I can do.' He added dourly, 'But I can't promise.'

Reading room? she thought as the door closed behind him. It was so dim in here, you'd probably go blind.

As she unfastened her damp trench coat, she looked around at the formal groups of hard leather armchairs and the table in the centre with magazines and periodicals arranged in regimented rows. They looked as if their cover stories might relate to Queen Victoria's jubilee, she thought, her mouth twisting.

Stationed round the walls were several glass-fronted bookcases with elaborate locks, but no keys, as if to discourage any attempt to open them, let alone prise out one of the rigid leather-bound volumes they contained.

The whole room seemed as if it had been frozen in time—or was that only because she felt the same? Numb, as if the world had stopped six hours ago when she'd looked at a line on a plastic tube, and seen it turn blue.

'Harry.' She whispered the name into the emptiness. 'Harry, you've got to help me. I don't know what to do.'

She heard the door open behind her and spun round in instinctive relief. But it was short-lived. Because the newcomer wasn't Harry. It was someone she'd never seen before. Someone taller, and much darker than Harry, but by no means as handsome, she thought, apprehension uncurling inside her. Harry had charm, and a smile that could melt icebergs. This man's mouth looked as if it had been forged from steel.

In addition, he had hair as black as a witch's cat, and the coldest blue eyes she'd ever seen. Which were currently looking her over with unconcealed exasperation.

'Oh, God.' His voice was low-pitched with a faint drawl. Perhaps a trace of an accent too. 'Who had the bright idea of inviting you, sweetheart? Because I'll wring his bloody neck.'

Jolted, she stared back at him. She said, 'I think there's some mistake. I'm here to see Harry Metcalfe.'

'I'm sure you are,' he said. 'But Harry's enjoying a bachelor dinner with some friends and relations, including his future father-in-law,' he added with a touch of grimness. 'So you can see that your intrusion would be completely inappropriate.' He reached into the jacket of his elegant suit and took out his wallet. 'How much to make you disappear?'

Her brows snapped together. She said, icily, 'I don't know who you are, but…'

'And I don't care who you are,' he cut across her, his tone bored. 'It's what you are that sticks in my gullet. Because it's really not that kind of party, so be a good girl, and don't hang around where you're not wanted.' He extracted some banknotes from his wallet. 'Now, tell me how much you were going to be paid, and add on the cab fare, so we can all get on with our lives.

'And it's nothing personal, darling.' The blue gaze skated over her again more slowly, taking in the simple knee-length black dress that her open raincoat revealed. His smile was swift and cynical. 'In other circumstances, I'd probably enjoy watching your performance. You might even persuade me to join in, if I'd had enough to drink. But this isn't your night, so I suggest you get off to your next engagement.'

She stared up at him, dazed, bewildered. She said thickly, 'What the hell are you talking about? I came here to see Harry, and I'm not leaving until I do.'

'Yes, you are,' he said. 'With a police escort, if necessary. Here.' He walked over to her, briskly peeling off some of the notes, and before she could read his intentions he pushed them down the front of her dress between her breasts, the long fingers casually brushing her rounded flesh.

She gave a small cry of outrage and stepped back, dragging out the money and throwing it at him.

She said hoarsely, 'How dare you—how dare you touch me— you bastard?'

'You mean touching's not part of the act?' He was unfazed, even mocking. 'Now, there's a novelty.' He paused for a moment, glancing towards the door. 'Oh, God,' he said wearily. 'The bloody cavalry. Just what I didn't want.'

The door was flung open and a younger man came in, sandy-haired and faintly flushed. 'I'm the search party, old boy,' he announced, faintly slurring his words. 'Your uncle Giles is asking for you.'

Then as his gaze discovered the room's other occupant he halted, and let out a long, slow whistle. 'You sly devil, you,' he said, grinning. 'Where did she come from?'

'How odd you should ask.' The drawl was even more pronounced. 'That, my dear Jack, was going to be my question— to you.'

Jack's brows lifted, and he began to laugh. 'You mean some live entertainment's arrived after all?' He raised his hands in mock surrender. 'Nothing to do with me, my friend. I seriously didn't dare, not when I heard your uncle Giles was planning to honour us with his presence. Couldn't see old Harry wanting to get his kit off and frolic with his bride's father looking on.'

He gave another appreciative whistle. 'But she's a bit adorable, eh? Not the usual type at all. Fancy giving a private show down here, darling? Just for the two of us?'

'No, she doesn't.' The retort from her adversary was clipped and immediate. 'You may be drunk enough, but I'm not. And anyway, we have a party to go back to, so she's leaving.'

He took her arm, but she wrenched herself free. 'Let go of me,' she said stormily, a hectic flush spreading along her cheekbones. 'You don't understand. This isn't—I'm not what you obviously think. I know Harry. I'm a friend of his, and I have to see him tonight—talk to him. It's terribly important.'

'Harry's friends are upstairs at his stag party,' he said. 'And you definitely weren't on the guest list. Now go.' He took her by the shoulders and turned her, pushing her inexorably towards the doorway.

She struggled against his grasp, aware of the raincoat slipping from her shoulders as they reached the hall. Her bag sliding away too, with the coat. Hitting the floor.

She reached down, trying to grab for it, and stumbled, almost sinking to her knees, but his fingers were like iron, pulling her up again.

The porter was on his feet, and there were other people there too—men—some of them on the stairs, but others right there in the hall, surrounding her, groping at her, trying to reach her zip, laughing and shouting, 'Off. Off.'

She felt the back of her dress tear, and cried out in fear. Knew the shock of her tormentors' hands on her bare skin.

And she suddenly saw Harry in the turmoil of grinning, hooting faces, standing towards the back. He was as white as a ghost, his mouth open in shock, staring at her as if she was his worst nightmare.

She called out to him, her voice high and desperate with panic. 'Harry—help me—please. You must...'

But he didn't move or speak. Only his expression changed, going from surprise to guilt. And from guilt, she realised, to cold fury.

It was then that she stopped fighting. That she let the hard male hands still on her shoulders propel her towards the club's open front door.

Where they halted. She found herself swung, not gently, to face him. She saw the blue eyes skim her with contempt, and, gasping, wrenched herself free of him at last, her naked skin feeling flayed where he'd touched her.

He took her coat and bag from the sandy-haired man, who'd appeared beside him, and tossed them to her.

He said softly and unsmilingly, 'I'd consider a change of career, darling, if you want to make a living. I don't think you're cut out for this.'

Then the door closed, leaving her outside in the rain-washed darkness, and more alone than she had ever been in her life.

CHAPTER ONE

Two years later

'MY FATHER retiring?' Darcy Langton gave a derisive snort. 'Only with the help of six pallbearers and a memorial service.'

'Darcy, dear,' her aunt said reproachfully. 'That's not nice. Not nice at all.'

Neither, thought Darcy, is my father, a lot of the time. But out of respect for her aunt Winifred, she didn't voice it aloud.

'Is this why I've been summoned home in such haste?' she demanded instead. 'To hear about his latest whim?'

Her aunt sighed. 'I think it's gone much further than that. He is actually standing down as managing director of Werner Langton, and plans to hand over as chairman too, just as soon as his successor finds his feet.'

'But there was no mention of this before I went away.' Darcy, who'd been standing by the window, staring at the sunlit autumn gardens, came back and seated herself on the sofa beside her aunt, stretching out slim, denim-clad legs. 'Yet, if it's this far advanced, he must have been planning it for ages.'

But then, she thought suddenly, we all have our secrets. Don't we?

Restlessly she flicked back a tendril of pale blonde hair that had escaped from the loose knot on top of her head.

She said abruptly, 'This successor you mentioned—has he already been appointed? Is he a member of the board?'

'No, he's not.' Aunt Freddie frowned slightly. 'In fact, he seems rather an odd choice. Much younger than I'd have expected.'

Darcy stared at her. 'You've met him, then?'

'Your father brought him down here a few weekends ago. They spent most of the time shut up in the study, so that must be when the deal was done.'

She shrugged. 'Your father seems very pleased with his choice. He says Werner Langton has become too complacent, and needs the injection of dynamism and drive that this young man will provide.'

'How on earth did they meet?'

'Your father went to the USA specially, because he'd heard of this whizkid who'd been there for the past year, troubleshooting various projects that had got into difficulties and turning them around.' She paused. 'His name is Joel Castille. Does that mean anything to you?'

Darcy shrugged. 'Absolutely not. It's quite an odd name, so I think I'd have remembered it.'

'It seems he had an English mother, but a French father.' Aunt Freddie devoted a moment to silent consideration. 'Quite striking looks, too. I don't do many portraits, as a rule, but he has a face I'd like to paint.'

Darcy's lips twitched faintly. 'Something to hang in the boardroom, maybe. You should suggest it to him.'

'No, darling,' Aunt Freddie said wryly. 'I really wouldn't dare—as you'll understand when you meet him. Your father's throwing a reception for him next week at the Templar Hotel. Introducing him to the company, and trade Press. And, naturally, he wishes you to act as his hostess for the occasion. You're so much better at these London things than I am.'

'Not true,' Darcy said instantly. 'You'd rather stay down here in your studio and paint than work the room at a party, or make polite conversation at formal dinners, that's all.

'But I see now why I've had the regal summons to return,' she added, her mouth tightening.

'Not altogether.' Her aunt spoke with a certain constraint. 'I'm afraid pictures of the police raid on the yacht appeared in some of the papers here—and you were clearly visible in them, and mentioned in the stories as one of Drew Maidstone's companions on board. Gavin is—not pleased. And that's putting it mildly.'

'Then it's a pity the Press—and Gavin—can't get their facts straight,' Darcy said hotly. 'Firstly, yes—there was a raid, and we all spent a few hours in custody while they searched the boat. No, it wasn't pleasant, but the search found nothing—no drugs or anything else untoward. It was a mistake.

'Secondly, I've been working on *Sorceress* and damned hard too. Drew doesn't bother with the charming playboy image when he's paying the wages, believe me,' she added bitterly. 'Nor was I sharing his stateroom—ever. I was squashed into something the size of a half-pint broom cupboard.'

She spread her hands. 'He just likes posh totty waiting on his guests, that's all. And he reckons I qualify.

'Thirdly, he was furious when I left, so Daddy will be pleased to hear I won't be going back, because I no longer have a job. I hope he's satisfied.'

'No, I don't think he will be,' Aunt Freddie said calmly. 'He wants to see you in some settled occupation, dearest, not skivvying round Europe and the Caribbean for frankly chancy characters like Mr Maidstone.'

'No,' Darcy said flatly, and with candour. 'He really wants to see me a boy—the son he never had, but always thought Mummy would give him eventually. The son who would have taken over from him at Werner Langton. Kept the dynasty going.' She shook her head. 'He never wanted a daughter—hadn't a clue what to do with me. And still hasn't.'

'You're very hard on him.' Her aunt spoke gently.

Darcy hunched a shoulder. 'It's mutual.'

'But things will not improve while you go out of your way to antagonise him.' Aunt Freddie spoke with unaccustomed severity. 'Werner Langton has been his life. Giving it up cannot have been an easy decision for him. So when he arrives, can we make a concerted effort to have a pleasant weekend?'

Darcy reached across and kissed her aunt on the cheek. 'For you—anything,' she said gently, and smiled.

But when she was alone, the smile faded. Much as she loved her aunt, it was galling to hear about the startling change in her father's future plans at second hand like this.

And if he hadn't suddenly needed her to be his hostess at the reception next week, because Aunt Freddie had jibbed, he wouldn't have sent for her, she thought bitterly. She'd simply have arrived home at some time in the future to discover a *fait accompli.*

He's not that different from Drew Maidstone, she told herself drily. He also needs some posh totty to wait on his guests. That's why I went on that course in France two years ago, to learn how to cook, and arrange flowers, and organise a household. Because I'm a girl, and to Dad, that's what girls are for. Or partly.

And if I hadn't been feeling so totally hellish, I might have fought back. Demanded some training where I could have used my brain. Had a proper career. But I simply didn't have the strength. Not then. Besides, I just wanted to get away—to escape.

She squared her shoulders. But that was all in the past, where it belonged. Dead and buried, with no looking back.

It was much more important to consider what the future might hold, she thought with slight unease. There was no doubt that her father's unexpected decision would bring about a big shake-up in all their lives.

Perhaps when he retired altogether, and would no longer need her services even marginally, she could get some proper qualifications at last. Up to now, her father's frequent calls on her had precluded her working on anything but a temporary basis, or performing much more than menial tasks that could be swiftly abandoned.

She might, she thought longingly, eventually find employment that would be more fulfilling and absorbing than acting as au pair for spoiled children, or cooking on board yachts which were basically extensions of the latest fashionable night clubs.

Maybe achieve something that would include real travel too.

The world could be opening up for her at last.

Hey there, Darcy, she whispered inwardly, abruptly halting her train of thought. You're running too far ahead of yourself here. Dad might change his mind about retirement—especially if this whizkid turns out to be a little too whizzy after all. You could be back at square one.

But maybe she could hope—just a little. After all, she told herself, you never know in life what might be just around the corner—do you?

* * *

It was a difficult weekend. Her father arrived looking dour, and insisted on seeing Darcy alone in his study soon afterwards.

'I hope you realise the Werner Langton Press office received calls from gutter journalists about the company you keep,' was his opening salvo. 'At every lunch I go to, other men are showing me pictures of their grandchildren. And what can I offer in return? My daughter being arrested in a drugs raid.'

Darcy bit her lip. 'The police searched the boat and found nothing,' she repeated wearily. 'No one was charged with anything.'

'More by luck than judgement,' her father returned angrily. 'Understand this, Darcy: I will not have you consorting with the likes of Drew Maidstone.'

She looked back at him stonily. 'I was his employee, Dad. Part of the crew, and nothing more.'

'And that's hardly to your credit either—being at the beck and call of that kind of riff-raff.' Under the thick thatch of silver hair, his face was unbecomingly flushed.

'But it's OK for me to put on a designer dress and smile at the people you do business with,' she said. 'Isn't that why I'm here now?'

He grunted. 'That's hardly the same thing. They know you're my daughter, and they treat you with respect. And that's how it should be, if you're ever to find a husband.'

She hadn't been expecting that. Her head went back. 'I'm hardly on the shelf at twenty.'

'Many more Drew Maidstone episodes and you'll be looked on as damaged goods. Is that what you want?'

She was very still suddenly, remembering contemptuous blue eyes judging her—stripping her...

Not, she thought, shivering inwardly, not twice in a lifetime.

'It's time you pulled yourself together, Darcy,' Gavin Langton went on. 'Began to take your life seriously. God knows what your mother would say to you if she was here now,' he added sombrely.

His previous remark had made her vulnerable. The cruelty of this left her gasping, but she rallied. 'She'd be saying nothing, because I wouldn't actually be present. I'd be away, starting my final year at university with her blessing and encouragement.'

'Of course,' he said with heavy sarcasm. 'Some ludicrous degree in engineering, wasn't it? To be followed by a job with the company, no doubt.'

He snorted. 'You think I'd allow my daughter to strut round on site in a hard hat, giving orders while the men laughed at you behind your back?'

'No,' she said, quietly. 'I—never thought that. But I hoped you might let me make—some contribution.'

'Then you can, at the reception next week. I want to make sure the evening goes smoothly. Not everyone approves of the man I've chosen to step into my shoes. Some of them feel…passed over, others are afraid the axe is going to fall, so I'll need you to…defuse any troublesome situations that might arise. After all, the shareholders won't like open warfare.'

'No,' she said, and hesitated. 'Why are you doing this, Dad? You're still years off retirement age. You could have introduced this man at a lower level. At least let him prove himself, before you give him the top job.'

'I've given my whole life to Werner Langton.' His voice was suddenly harsh. 'Travelled the world building bridges, digging tunnels, putting up shopping malls. I was in Venezuela when your mother died. I've thought a thousand times that if I'd been here, I might have been able to do something. That she could still be with us now.

'I plan to enjoy the time that's left to me.' He gave a grim smile. 'Let the company swallow up another willing sacrifice. I've paid my dues. And Joel Castille will follow me, whatever the rest of them think.'

She said slowly, 'It didn't occur to you to speak to me first— talk things over.'

'And you'd have advised me, would you—out of your vast experience?' He shook his head. 'I make my own decisions. Just be pleasant to my choice of managing director, Darcy, and see the evening goes smoothly. That's your forte.'

He looked her over, his lips pursing irritably at the jeans and sweatshirt she was wearing. 'And buy yourself a new dress— something glamorous that'll make you look like a woman. Don't forget you have a bad impression to wipe away.'

She felt her hands tighten into fists, but made herself unclench them. Even smile. 'Yes, Father,' she said quietly. 'Of course.'

'The guest of honour is late,' Aunt Freddie murmured. 'And your father is getting agitated.'

'Not my problem,' Darcy returned softly, smiling radiantly over her untouched glass of champagne. 'He can't expect me to go out and scour the highways and byways for the guy.' She paused. 'Perhaps he knows there's dissension in the ranks over his appointment, and has changed his mind.'

Her aunt shuddered faintly. 'Don't even think it. Can you imagine the fallout?'

'Yes, but at least you're here to help me cope. I'm truly grateful, Freddie. I know how you hate London.'

'But occasionally, a visit is inevitable.' Her aunt looked around her, and sighed. 'What a disagreeable evening. All these resentful faces.'

'Plus a drunken waiter, and a waitress spilling a tray of canapés all over the finance director's wife,' Darcy reminded her softly.

'They may turn out to be the high spots of the party.' Aunt Freddie turned to survey her niece. 'You look very lovely, darling, but does it always have to be black?'

Darcy glanced down at her figure-skimming voile dress, with its narrow straps and the bias-cut skirt that swirled as she moved.

'This is a compromise,' she said. 'I was looking for sackcloth and ashes.'

'Well, start celebrating instead,' her aunt said with open relief. 'Because the errant guest has finally made it.' She sighed deeply. 'Oh, for a sketch pad.'

Amused, Darcy turned towards the doorway. A group of Werner Langton executives was already clustering round the latecomer, and, for a moment, her view was blocked by her father's commanding figure.

She ought to join them, she thought. Play her part in the meeting and greeting.

She took a step, then the group shifted, and she saw him. And, sick with shock, recognised him. Confronted the harrowing, unforgettable image she'd carried for two years—the tall figure with black hair, and eyes as cold as a northern sea in his tanned face.

Not a bad dream or a hallucination. But here—now—in this room—breathing the same air. And looking round him.

Almost, she thought, dry-mouthed, as if he was searching for someone…

CHAPTER TWO

DARCY COULDN'T move. Could barely think straight.

She gulped air. Any other social event, and she could have contrived to vanish discreetly. But not this one. Not tonight. There was no way.

She tried desperately to compose herself. To be rational.

He won't remember, she tried to tell herself frantically. Why should he? It was two years ago, for heaven's sake, in a dimly lit room. She'd changed since then, she was slimmer, had different hair. She was older.

And he wouldn't be expecting to see her either.

But, as their eyes met at last across the room, Darcy found herself reeling under a look that froze her flesh to her backbone.

For a heartbeat she was stunned, then she lifted her chin and returned the look with as much additional venom as she could muster.

Only to realise, with horror, that he was actually crossing the room towards her. Standing straight in front of her, when he must know, if he possessed a grain of sense or tact, that she would never want to see or speak to him again.

That the looks they'd exchanged had said it all.

She was aware of Aunt Freddie's surprised glance at her as the taut silence lengthened, then her quiet voice saying, 'Mr Castille, how nice to see you again. I don't think you've met my niece. Darcy, this is Werner Langton's new managing director, Joel Castille.'

She was prepared to bluff it out. To take the only option—shake hands and turn away.

But he was not.

He said softly, 'Actually, Miss Langton and I have met before, but only briefly. It was two years ago, around the time of Harry Metcalfe's wedding. I'm sure she remembers.'

'No,' Darcy returned with total and chilling clarity. 'I do not.'

'Are you sure it was the Metcalfe wedding?' Aunt Freddie was wrinkling her brow. 'Because none of us actually attended it. We were invited as neighbours, of course, but only out of politeness, I'm sure. And Darcy was in London, staying with friends.' She turned to the unsmiling statue beside her. 'You were ill there, weren't you, darling? A severe migraine, if I recall. Such a shame.'

'A shame, indeed,' Joel Castille said gravely. There were twin devils dancing in the cold blue eyes. 'Do you suffer much from migraines, Miss Langton?'

'As a matter of fact,' she said, 'I feel as if I might be developing one right now.'

'And we didn't meet at the wedding itself,' he added, turning to her aunt. 'But at one of the parties beforehand. Isn't that right, Miss Langton?'

'Your memory is clearly better than mine,' she said icily. 'I have no recollection of you at all, Mr Castille.'

'What a pity,' he said lightly. 'Now, I found our encounter electrifying—quite unforgettable.' His eyes went over her with that same sensual male appraisal that she'd never quite been able to erase from her mind. The look that suggested she was standing in front of him, unclothed. His loaded smile seemed to leave a bruise. 'And I look forward to renewing our acquaintance.'

As he moved away, Aunt Freddie said in quiet reproach, 'Darcy, what were you thinking of? You were almost rude to Mr Castille.'

Rude? thought Darcy, shock now battling with fury inside her. I'm only sorry I didn't kick him where it hurts, and throw up all over his shoes.

She said shortly, 'I didn't find him quite as irresistible as he clearly does himself.' She shrugged. 'But, what the hell? Hopefully, we won't have to meet again.' Please God. *Please God.*

The evening became like some weird game of hide-and-seek,

she thought afterwards. She tried to be totally unobtrusive. He let her know, without coming near her, that he knew exactly where she was at any given moment. And she flinched under that knowledge.

At the same time, he could work a room, she acknowledged without pleasure. She could actually notice a thaw in the atmosphere. Realised that some tight-lipped expressions had relaxed. That people were approaching him, gathering round him, wanting to talk. And that he was listening.

She saw her father smiling expansively, not even bothering to conceal his triumph that the first hurdle, at least, had been cleared with consummate ease.

But she found her own heart sinking.

It was ludicrous to hope that her desperate prayer would be answered, and that Joel Castille could simply be—dismissed from her life, as if he'd never existed. He was only too real. And letting her know it, too.

She heard some sally from her father and the quieter response, followed by an appreciative roar of laughter, and winced. Langton and Castille, she thought, grabbing another glass of champagne from a passing tray. The new double act.

I'll be lucky if my father doesn't offer to adopt him.

Oh, God, if I could just get out of here. If I didn't have to stay until the bitter end.

Instinct told her that she hadn't heard the last of him. That he would seek her out again before the night was over. But at least this time she would be slightly more prepared.

She'd just said goodnight to the personnel director and his wife when Joel Castille eventually came up to her. She took an instinctive step backwards, which was a mistake because it took her into a corner, and she found herself blocked there, her only escape route to push right past him.

She stood her ground and waited.

He said softly, 'You have no idea how much I've been looking forward to this evening.'

'Of course.' She didn't even pretend to smile. Her expression was stone, and to hell with what people thought. 'You've just landed one of the top jobs in the industry. Congratulations. Now leave me alone.'

'I really didn't know you were Gavin's daughter,' he went on as if she hadn't spoken. 'Until I saw that photograph of you adorning the grand piano in the drawing room at Kings Whitnall. You looked younger, of course, and more innocent, but quite unmistakable.'

His gaze roamed over her, slowly and comprehensively. 'And tonight you're wearing black again. But then it's your colour. Gives that lovely skin of yours the sheen of ivory. I recollect thinking that at our last encounter. Besides, white would hardly be appropriate, would it?'

'If you say so.'

Black, she thought, was a non-colour. It was darkness—it was mourning. It was a vast hole in the middle of the universe, filled with nothing.

He'd paused, deliberately building up the tension that already vibrated between them. 'Of course, Harry said you were a neighbour's daughter, and I knew whereabouts he lived, so I should have put two and two together.'

'And made five, no doubt,' she said. 'Like last time.'

'Listen, darling,' he said. 'Pretty blondes who turn up at stag nights are asking to be misunderstood. Anyway, I wasn't so far off the mark,' he added sardonically. 'You might not have been a stripper, but you were still trouble. One look at Harry's face told me that.'

Harry's face. Oh, God, Harry's face…

She rallied. 'And what gave you the right to interfere?'

'His wife is my cousin, Emma.' His tone hardened. 'I've known her since she was a tot, and I care very deeply about her happiness. Harry Metcalfe wouldn't have been my choice for her, but she—loves him. So, I wasn't going to have her wedding ruined by a spoiled, man-hungry little bitch like you.'

She was white to the lips. 'How dare you? You know nothing—nothing about me.'

He said grimly, 'The bridegroom told me all I needed to know—after some persuasion. He said that you'd had a crush on him for years, and you'd always been hanging around him, trying to attract his attention. Do you deny it?'

'No.' Her voice was almost inaudible.

I was a child. And he was like a god to me—gorgeous, glamorous Harry. I'd had hopes—dreams. Who wouldn't? And, of course, I wanted to be noticed by him—but not like that. Not ever like that...

'Eventually, against his better judgement, you had a brief fling together,' the hard voice went on. 'He admitted that. Also that he knew he'd made a terrible mistake, and just wanted to forget the whole thing, only you wouldn't allow that—would you, beautiful? You refused to let go.

'He said that you'd been making a nuisance of yourself ever since, phoning and sending text messages. In effect— stalking him. That you had this pathetic obsession with him and were begging him to break it off with Emma, and marry you instead.'

Darcy drew a deep, unsteady breath. 'And, of course, you believed him?'

'Why not? I'd seen for myself how persistent you could be.' The cold eyes were contemptuous. 'Are you now saying you didn't have sex with Harry—that he invented it?'

'No.' She looked down at the floor. 'I—can't say that. And I knew he had a girlfriend, because he always did. But I didn't know he was going to be married. Not until the wedding invitations arrived,' she added, almost inaudibly.

'But it was true that you'd been trying to contact him before you came to the club that night? That you wouldn't take no for an answer?'

'Yes.'

I wanted to know how he could have done what he did—with me—when he was in love with someone else. Engaged to her. I needed to ask why—that's all.

Then I realised our so-called 'fling' was going to have consequences, and I was scared—so scared. I didn't know what to do—who else to turn to. Was that so wrong?

'And you were trying to stop the wedding?' His voice probed at her again.

'Yes—I—I suppose so.'

Was I? I can barely remember any more. I think I just needed Harry to listen—to take some responsibility for what he'd done.

But what I do recall is those men's faces—sweating, gloating. And you—your hands on me... That I remember most of all.

'Then I'm glad you didn't get away with it,' he said curtly, 'because it would have broken Em's heart, and that's not allowed, whatever my private take on Harry.'

'Fine,' Darcy said quietly and savagely. 'It's all over, and no harm done, so can we leave it there? Because you've had your say, Mr Castille. You've raked up a lot of things I'd rather forget about, and I'd really like it to stop. Besides, people are leaving, and I need to say goodnight to them.'

'Of course,' he said. 'Daddy's only daughter. The perfect hostess.' His mouth twisted. 'My God, if he only knew.'

'Let's leave him in his innocence, shall we?' She stared back in challenge. 'Like your cousin Emma?'

She made to get past him, but he halted her, his hand on her arm. 'One moment. I hope you don't still harbour any obsessive little fantasies about Harry? Because that could make your life awkward.'

She shook him off almost violently. 'You—do—not touch me.' She choked out the words. 'Not now. Not ever. And my sole fantasy, Mr Castille, is never to see you again as long as I live.'

'Unfortunate,' he said. 'Because something tells me that we shall be meeting again, and quite soon. So, let's simply bow to the inevitable, shall we? And smile while we're doing it,' he added softly. 'Or people might notice.'

He looked down at her again, in slow assessment, and she saw the hard mouth soften, curve into deliberate amusement—and something more.

Because his smile did several strange things to her, none of which she wanted to happen. To her utter horror and dismay, it seemed to smooth an errant strand of hair back from her face, kiss her mouth gently and delicately caress the tips of her breasts.

Suddenly her heart was racing, and she felt her pale skin burn. And he knew it. The smile told her that too.

She hastily strengthened her wavering defences, gave him a look of pure loathing and walked away. At the same time, wondering, with every step she took, if he was watching her go.

* * *

'I saw you having a long chat to Joel,' Gavin Langton commented with satisfaction. He was standing, brandy glass in hand, before the fireplace in the drawing room of their Chelsea house. He nodded. 'You did well tonight, Darcy. Very well.'

'Thank you.' She kept her voice neutral. Yet her heart was still thudding unnaturally, and she felt hollow inside.

She'd wanted to go straight to bed when they got back, and Aunt Freddie had already done so, but, as usual, her father wanted to talk about the evening's events over coffee, and a nightcap.

'So, what did you think of him?'

She made a deliberate effort not to stiffen. Even managed to speak relatively lightly. 'I thought my role was purely decorative. That I wasn't required to have an opinion. Or, at least, not to voice it.'

Her father frowned. 'You're a pretty girl. He's a good-looking man. There must have been some reaction.'

Yes, she thought, there was. But not one I'd ever wish to contemplate. I think I must have gone a little mad.

'He was the guest of honour.' She shrugged. 'I thought you'd want me to be civil. But I doubt we'll ever be friends.'

She was still shaking at the memory of those last minutes in his company. She felt incensed by the way he'd looked at her. Degraded.

'Oh?' He looked at her sharply. 'And why's that, pray?'

She replaced her cup carefully in its saucer. 'Well—I have very little contact with the company, so the opportunity will hardly arise.'

'I wouldn't be too sure of that. Joel's been in America for the past eighteen months, so I plan to do more entertaining—make sure he's properly introduced around. Also, it seems he might be visiting regularly in our neighbourhood in Hampshire.'

'Oh,' Darcy said. 'Why?'

Her father pursed his lips. 'Harry Metcalfe and his wife are coming back from Malaysia quite soon, and moving in at the Hall with his parents while they look for a house of their own.'

There was a sudden buzzing in Darcy's ears, and her mouth went dry.

'I didn't know that,' she managed somehow.

Her father nodded. 'Joel's related to Emma Metcalfe, of course. First cousins, apparently, but he looks on her more as his younger sister. Speaks of her with great affection. And he's concerned about her, too. The climate abroad didn't suit her, apparently, particularly now she's having a baby. So naturally he feels protective.'

The world seemed to dissolve around her. Slide sideways, turning crimson with a pain she'd thought buried forever. If she hadn't been sitting down, she might have fallen. *A baby...*

She heard herself say from some great distance, 'So she has two men watching out for her—her husband, and her cousin. Lucky girl.'

'Perhaps.' Her father's frown deepened. 'I never had a lot of time for young Metcalfe. Definite lightweight, I thought. Oh, I knew you had some childish thing about him once, but I was always glad that he never came sniffing round you.'

'Yes,' she said. 'It was just as well he had Emma.'

She wished she could appreciate the terrible, unspeakable irony of it all, but it was impossible. She longed only to crawl away into some dark, forgotten corner, and deal with her grief all over again. Something she'd believed she would not have to do.

Her father was speaking again. 'Things are going to be changing, Darcy. Changing rapidly for all of us, and maybe it's time you and I talked seriously about the future.'

She steadied herself, kept her voice even. 'I'd like that. But not now, please. Not tonight. I'm a bit whacked.'

'You've not recovered from burning the candle at both ends on that damned boat, I suppose,' he said gruffly, then relented. 'Off with you, then, my child.'

He walked across to her and dropped a kiss on the top of her head. 'I was proud of you tonight,' he said. 'I want to go on feeling like that.'

She gave him half a smile, and fled.

Safely in her room, she threw herself face downward across the bed and stayed there. How could one short evening bring so many disasters? she asked herself in agonised disbelief. And what the hell could she do to prevent any more occurring? It seemed to her that she was trapped between the devil and the deep blue sea.

If she stayed in London, it would be difficult to avoid Werner Langton's new managing director completely, as she needed to do. Particularly as her father seemed determined to be involved with him socially as well.

Whereas if she went down to Kings Whitnall, sooner or later Harry would turn up, with his wife. His pregnant wife.

Was that why she'd received that oblique warning from Joel Castille? Could he really think she still cherished memories of Harry? Well, he seemed to have swallowed all Harry's half-truths, lies and evasions, so he probably did.

She shuddered and sat up, pushing her dishevelled hair back from her face. Across the room, her mirror reflected a white-faced, wild-eyed creature she barely recognised.

She pulled off her dress, and tossed it aside with loathing as she walked to the bathroom. No more black ever, she swore to herself, recoiling at the memory of Joel Castille's gaze making its lingering way down her body.

Tomorrow she would go back to the agency she used and find another job as an au pair. Lisbon, maybe, or Vienna, she thought. Or even—Australia.

It wasn't at all what she'd hoped for, of course.

She cleaned off her make-up, and stepped under the shower, welcoming the sting of the water on her overheated skin.

But maybe it was time to stop dreaming about careers she would never have, and face up to reality.

And the truth was, she needed to get as far away as possible, and as soon as possible. So, she would have to settle for whatever was available.

She dried herself, slipped into a nightdress and went back into the bedroom. She felt stifled suddenly, so she went over to open the window. It had begun to rain, she realised, and the glass panes were running with water, but she undid the catch anyway and pushed the frame a few inches ajar, allowing a draught of cold, dank city air to penetrate the room.

She climbed into bed, pulling the covers up around her shoulders with a faint shiver.

Traffic noise in London had never bothered her particularly, and their square was quiet enough. And when the distant rumble of cars and buses was conjoined with the splash of the rain, it was almost soporific.

She hadn't expected to sleep, yet she did, only to find herself dreaming endlessly of rain-washed pavements and a flight of steps leading to a door that would not open to her, however hard she knocked for admittance. And she woke in the grey dawn light with tears on her face.

Darcy pulled off her black blazer, and tossed it over the back of the sofa with her bag, before sinking down onto the cushions and kicking off her shoes. She rested for a moment, flexing her aching toes with a slight grimace. She must have walked miles, she thought, and what had she achieved? Practically zilch.

The au pair market was crowded by eager and cheaper applicants from Eastern Europe. The only post immediately available was one she'd actually taken a year ago with an American couple living in Paris, who believed their three hyperactive children should grow up with total freedom from discipline and who had since, Darcy heard with horror, been blessed with a fourth hostage to liberty. No one, the agency had frankly confessed, would stay for longer than a week. A situation that Darcy totally understood.

She had tried other agencies, and even job centres, but without success.

'I really want to work abroad,' she'd said wearily as she was offered yet another computer training course.

The girl behind the desk had given her an old-fashioned look. 'Don't we all?' she'd responded crisply.

Which wasn't a great deal of help.

She hoped Aunt Freddie had met with better luck in whatever business had brought her to the city. She'd been almost mysterious about it at breakfast, declining Darcy's offer to meet her for lunch with the excuse that she wasn't sure of her plans.

So what was that all about? Darcy wondered.

Her reverie was interrupted by the quiet voice of their housekeeper, Mrs Inman. 'I thought I heard you come in, Miss

Langton. I wondered if you'd take a quick look at the dining room, and approve the table settings before you go up to change.'

Darcy glanced down at her white silk blouse, and corded damson skirt. Quite good enough for a simple family supper, she decided. Mrs Inman was a treasure, but not over-confident about her abilities, and inclined to fuss a little over non-essentials.

She said gently, 'There's only the three of us, Mrs Inman, and I'm sure everything looks lovely.'

'Well, if you're quite certain. Only your father seemed to think…' The other woman's voice tailed off as she gave a swift, nervous smile and left the room.

Darcy curled up, unfastening the button at the neck of her blouse, plus a couple more for good measure, and tucking her stockinged feet under her. It had been a pretty dispiriting day, she mused, leaning back and closing her eyes, but maybe things would be better tomorrow. They certainly couldn't get any worse.

Her mind was beginning to drift, and she was almost sinking into a tired doze, when she suddenly heard the sound of the door bell. She sat up, surprised, glancing at her watch, wondering who on earth could be calling at this hour. Unless, of course, Aunt Freddie had forgotten her key again. It had been known.

As the drawing-room door opened she turned her head casually, ready to make some teasing comment, and froze as she saw Joel Castille walk into the room.

He paused, his brows lifting sardonically as he registered her horrified expression. 'Good evening.' His voice was silky, but the note of faint amusement was unmistakable.

Darcy shot upright, her feet frantically scrabbling for her discarded shoes. 'What the hell are you doing here?' she demanded hoarsely.

He had the audacity to smile. 'Don't look now, sweetheart,' he drawled. 'But I think you've just blown your perfect-hostess image. Didn't you know that your father had invited me to dinner?'

'No,' she said curtly. 'Obviously not.' She badly wanted to re-fasten those damned buttons on her shirt, which he'd already noticed, but knew that would only give him further ammunition.

'I wonder why not,' he said pensively. 'Maybe he thought you might suddenly remember a previous engagement.'

'And he'd have been right,' Darcy said stonily. Shod once more, she got to her feet. 'You'll both have to excuse me, I'm afraid. But I'm sure you have a lot to talk about. I'd only be in the way.'

As she made for the door he halted her, his fingers closing on her arm.

She pulled free, glaring at him. 'Do not—ever—put your hands on me again.'

He stepped back, lifting them in mock-surrender. 'Just a word of warning, Miss Langton. I don't think your father would be pleased if you disappeared this evening. He seems to want us to be friends.'

'Something else he hasn't chosen to mention.' She lifted her chin. 'Why didn't you tell him he's wasting his time?'

'Because it seemed a little arbitrary. And it occurred to me that for the sake of future harmony, you and I could perhaps develop—a working relationship. On a temporary basis only, of course. Until his retirement is complete.'

She shook her head, angrily aware that his blue gaze had returned to the loosened front of her shirt. 'No, Mr Castille,' she said. 'Not even for the space of the next five minutes.'

'A pity,' he said. 'Your father doesn't strike me as a man who takes disappointment well. It's something we have in common,' he added levelly.

'Then that's as far as the resemblance goes,' she said. 'And if he had any idea how you once treated me, you'd be looking for another job.'

'Which I'd find,' he said. 'How's your employment record, Miss Langton? Logged on the police computer?'

Her face was suddenly burning. 'How dare you?'

'Well, it's hardly a secret.' He shrugged. 'Drew Maidstone is pretty notorious, and you're extremely photogenic. And as we're being totally frank, you should be grateful to me. I got you away from that party two years ago just in time. People had been drinking, and things could have turned nasty for you. I'm sure you remember that.'

'I remember,' she said, 'that as far as I was concerned, you were just one more animal in a truly disgusting pack. So, gratitude doesn't really feature.'

He wasn't smiling any more, and she saw a muscle flicker at the corner of his mouth. She'd got to him at last, she thought, and knew a fleeting moment of triumph.

'All the same,' he said, after a pause, 'you might be wiser to stay at home for dinner tonight.'

'And if ever I need your advice,' she said, 'I'll ask for it.' She collected blazer and bag, and walked past him into the hall.

She was at the front door when her father's voice reached her. 'Darcy? Where are you going?'

She turned to see him coming down the stairs, his expression faintly forbidding.

'To visit Lois.' She kept her tone light. 'Pizza, a bottle of wine and a couple of chicks' movies. Didn't I say?'

'No, it must have slipped your mind.' He gave her a sharp look. 'And I'm afraid you must telephone Lois and make your excuses. As you now know, we have a guest, and I need you here this evening to act as my hostess.'

'Aunt Freddie seems to be one of Mr Castille's fans,' she returned defiantly. 'I'm sure she'd take my place for once.'

'Your aunt returned to Kings Whitnall this afternoon. I pay you a generous allowance, Darcy, and occasionally I expect you to earn it.' He waited, giving a nod as, reluctantly, she turned back from the door. 'Now, run upstairs and tidy yourself, then join us for sherry,' he added implacably, ignoring her pleading look.

Mutinously, Darcy went to her room. She washed her face and hands, then applied moisturiser, but no other cosmetics. Not even a touch of her favourite scent. No concessions whatsoever, she told herself, brushing her hair vigorously then sweeping it back severely from her face, in order to confine it, with a silver clip, at the nape of her neck.

Mouth tightening, she refastened her shirt to the throat, and straightened her skirt.

Then she took a deep, steadying breath, trying to calm the flurried beat of her heart, and went slowly and unhappily down to the drawing room, and the continuing nightmare that waited for her there.

CHAPTER THREE

SHE'D EXPECTED to be met with a combination of mockery and triumph, but she was wrong. Joel Castille rose politely as she entered, his smile pleasant and unchallenging, then brought her the glass of excellent *amontillado* that she'd requested in a small wooden voice.

Then he and her father resumed their quiet conversation, and she was left, thankfully, to her own devices.

But, with her enemy sitting only a few feet away, long legs stretched in front of him, dark face warmly alive as he talked, it was difficult to divorce herself as totally from the proceedings as she might wish. He was speaking about some project he'd been involved with in Colombia, and the inbuilt problems his team had been forced to overcome, and she was annoyed to find her attention first captured, then engaged.

In addition, as time passed, Darcy realised uneasily that she was studying him covertly under her lashes, taking in the elegant lines of the charcoal suit, and the way its waistcoat accentuated his lean body. Her aunt had mentioned he had a French father, and she saw that particular heritage in the occasional swift, graceful gesture of the long-fingered hands when he wished to emphasise some point.

Attractive? Well, yes, she was forced, grudgingly, to admit. But not in any way that could ever appeal to her, although if Lois ever got to see him she would probably describe him as sex on legs.

But even without the events of two years before, Darcy would always find a man like Joel Castille eminently resistible. He was too armoured in his own arrogance, she told herself. His sense of power.

Joel Castille was clearly brilliant at his job, and a born raconteur, but it would be a relief when her father finally retired, bringing this interregnum to an end. Then she could finally airbrush his successor out of sight, mind and memory.

But long before that happy day, she needed to remove herself completely from his sphere of influence, she thought, and found herself suddenly wondering why she should know that with such total conviction. And also such terrifying urgency.

Fool, she castigated herself. It's not that difficult to work out. You have to get away before something is said, deliberately or by chance, which could bring all your skeletons from two years ago tumbling into the open. Some random comment that will give your father the idea that you and Joel Castille have some kind of shared past, because that would be a disaster.

And the prospect of Harry coming back just increases the pressure. Because it would be so easy if he wished to make mischief...

She closed her mind at this point. She couldn't let herself think about that, she told herself fiercely.

She simply needed to stay cool, and take the necessary avoiding action. And then everything would be fine. Or at least survivable.

Tomorrow she'd make it clear to the agency that she'd take any job at all, even if it meant, heaven help her, going back to Paris to the Harrisons and their demonic brood, and hoping that some other alternative opportunity for employment would present itself while she was there, and before she was driven either mad, or to murder.

She realised suddenly that a momentary silence had fallen, and that both men were looking at her, Joel's eyes intent and slightly narrowed.

Her father said, rather too heartily, 'I've been telling Joel how beautiful the woods round Kings Whitnall are looking— with the autumn tints. We'll have to persuade him to come down again and see for himself.'

'Mr Castille is a much travelled man,' she said coolly, avoiding that too searching gaze. 'I don't think a few autumn leaves are enough to interest him.'

'I'm always fascinated by beauty, Miss Langton,' he drawled. 'Wherever it may be found. And whatever unlikely form it takes,' he added softly.

She was aware of her hands involuntarily clenching into fists, and was rescued by Mrs Inman, who came to say that dinner was served.

The housekeeper had always been an excellent cook, but that night she seemed to have surpassed herself. Her wonderful thick vegetable soup was followed by rib of beef, succulently pink in the middle, served with crisp golden potatoes and an array of vegetables, perfectly cooked. For dessert there was Queen of Puddings, served with a bowl of whipped cream.

And when she came to clear the plates, and tell them coffee would be served in the drawing room, she accepted Joel Castille's sincere praise with shy, pink-faced pleasure.

Darcy had not felt like eating, but she knew that any failure of appetite on her part would be noted and commented on by her father, so she'd forced the food down as if she'd been programmed to do so.

Now that it was too late, she realised she'd been a fool to let Joel Castille see that his re-entry into her life mattered to her one iota.

She should have smiled—shrugged the whole thing off. Maybe pretended it was a joke that had gone wrong. That she was one of a whole series of girls who were supposed to turn up and play tricks on Harry.

He might not have believed her, but if she'd stuck to her guns he'd have had to accept her story. And she could have edged her way out of the situation quietly, and without fuss.

In the meantime, this was turning into the pleasant social occasion from hell.

It was so difficult, she discovered, to be forced to converse with someone and maintain an essential distance at the same time. Especially when that someone seemed to have read many of the same books, seen some of the same films and liked much of the same music that she did herself. Or so he claimed, anyway.

Joel Castille was making himself agreeable, and she didn't want that. She wanted him to be brutal and bullying again. Behave in a way that would give her every excuse to shun him, and give her father every reason to accept those excuses.

She groaned inwardly. Oh, why had Aunt Freddie gone back to Kings Whitnall? Why wasn't she here to give her niece some respite from this unwanted charm offensive?

As it was, she could almost hear Gavin purring with satisfaction, and she wanted to scream in frustration and rage, because her tormentor was doing this quite deliberately. Putting her in an impossible position, and watching her squirm.

All right, she wanted to shout at him. I made a mistake once when I was eighteen, but I've suffered for it. And I don't need to be continually harassed and punished by you of all people. So, why the hell can't you leave me alone?

And she would have to sit there in the drawing room and take anything he cared to dish out, smiling politely as she did so. She couldn't even use one of her migraines as an excuse to quit this ghastly threesome, she realised bitterly. He'd see through that in an instant.

Yet it was Joel Castille himself who called a halt to her profound discomfort. He drank his coffee and rose to his feet.

'I hate to break up such an unforgettable evening,' he said, 'but I have an early start tomorrow, and a crowded day. Will you forgive me, please?'

'As long as you promise to dine here again very soon.' Gavin Langton clapped him on the shoulder. 'Show Joel to the door, won't you, darling?' he added to Darcy.

Only a few more minutes, she thought as she preceded him, sedate and unsmiling, to the front door. She held it open. 'Goodnight, Mr Castille.'

But he'd halted, and was looking down at her, smiling faintly.

He said, 'You look as if you're about to take the minutes of some meeting.' He glanced pointedly at the rigidly closed top button of her shirt. 'Now, I prefer the dishevelled look, with your hair loose and your dress falling off.'

The shiver that ran down her spine had little to do with the chill of the night air entering the hallway.

She said in a low, scornful voice, 'Your personal preferences are a matter of complete indifference to me. As far as I'm concerned, Mr Castille, you're in this house purely on sufferance.'

He remained unruffled. 'And has it ever occurred to you, Miss Langton,' he drawled, 'that the same might be said of you?'

He paused. 'Tell me something,' he said quietly. 'What exactly did you hope to achieve that night two years ago?'

She stiffened. 'That's none of your business.'

'Then indulge me,' he said. 'Satisfy my curiosity.'

'No.'

'Why not?'

'Because you know quite enough about me already.' She faced him, chin up, her grey-green eyes sparking furiously. 'I'm a marriage wrecker. A weapon of mass destruction. There's no need for more.'

'Now, there we differ.' He spoke softly, his blue gaze suddenly and disturbingly intense. 'Because I've only just begun to find out about you. And before I'm finished, I intend to discover everything there is to know. So, be warned.'

He went past her, and out into the night.

It was hardly a grand gesture to slam the door after him, but Darcy did it anyway. And found, as she'd suspected, that it was no comfort at all.

She went back to the drawing room to find her father had poured himself another brandy, and was seated, gazing broodingly into space. Perhaps it was a trick of the lamplight, but for a moment it seemed to Darcy as if his face was shadowed, even haggard.

But when he looked at her it was with his usual searching look, and the illusion passed. 'You took long enough to say goodnight.'

'On the contrary,' Darcy returned coolly. 'Mr Castille doesn't know when he's outstayed his welcome.'

'Speaking of which,' he said slowly, 'you might have taken a little more trouble with your appearance tonight.'

'When we have guests, I will.' There was a chill in her voice. 'Mr Castille already seems to be part of the family.'

'Maybe he is, at that.' He shook his head. 'Dear God, Darcy

when I'm talking to him, I see myself at the same age. He's just what Werner Langton needs.'

'Which I never could be, of course.' She didn't hide her bitterness. 'Why don't you say it, Daddy? He's the son you never had.'

'I'm not exactly in my dotage,' he came back at her sharply. 'There could yet be another Langton to take up the reins in the years to come. I've never taken a vow of celibacy, you know.'

'No,' she said. 'Of course not.'

Her thoughts were sober as she went up to bed. 'Another Langton', her father had said. Could he really be considering marrying again—spending his retirement with another woman—even starting a second family? Plenty of other men did so, of course.

But how would she feel about sharing her home with a stepmother, and having younger siblings around? Except it wouldn't be her home any more. And what on earth would Aunt Freddie do under those circumstances?

She'd put her career as an artist on hold when her sister, Darcy's mother, had died, and moved into Kings Whitnall, a gentle presence to run the house and care for a small, bewildered child.

As Darcy had grown older, she'd come to understand that her aunt cared far more deeply for Gavin than he seemed to realise.

He's probably so used to having her around that he doesn't see her any more—or not as a woman he could love, she thought sadly.

She hung her skirt in the wardrobe, and put the rest of her clothing in the laundry basket for Mrs Inman to attend to. The kind of luxury she would have to learn to do without, she told herself.

Kings Whitnall had always been her safety net. Somewhere to come home to. Safety and security under one welcoming roof. Now she might have to learn to be a guest there.

But if there was to be a new regime, at least she wouldn't have to deal with Joel Castille, she reflected as she slipped into bed. And for that she could be truly thankful.

Even so, Darcy suddenly found herself remembering the way he'd looked at her as he was leaving. Heard again the softly voiced promise that threatened what was left of her peace of mind. And dragged the bedclothes around her body, shivering.

On the spur of the moment, she went down to Kings Whitnall the following afternoon. She needed, she thought, to talk to Freddie. To lay the cards on the table. But there was a shock in store for her.

'Darcy, my love,' her aunt said, pouring tea in the drawing room. 'Please don't worry about me. I've been making my own plans. I'm not needed here any longer. So, I'm ready to move on.'

'But where will you go?' Darcy bit her lip. 'If I had a real job, we could find a flat, maybe. Somewhere together.' She sighed. 'But I haven't got any kind of work at the moment. I was thinking of going back to that awful family in Paris, but even they managed to find someone else while I was making up my mind. So I can't even afford a grotty bedsit right now.'

'Well, I wouldn't worry too much.' There was an odd note in her aunt's voice. 'I'm sure your father has plans for you. And I do have somewhere to go. I went up to London to sort out the final arrangements.'

She paused. 'You remember Barbara Lee, my great friend from school and art-college days? Well, she was appointed as headmistress of St Benedict's last year, and she's been looking for someone to teach art there.'

She drew a breath. 'I didn't say anything before, because I had to be interviewed by the board of governors. That's where I was yesterday, and they've offered me the job, and asked me to start next month. I'm so thrilled about it all. It's just the new beginning I need.'

Darcy said slowly, 'It all sounds wonderful.' And so it did. Her aunt sounded confident—energised. A different woman, taking her life by the throat.

I'm less than half her age, she reflected unhappily. And I feel as if everything around me has shifted by about sixty degrees and I don't know where I am any more. Or where I can go next.

And she knew exactly who was responsible for this turmoil in her existence.

Damn you, Joel Castille, she thought savagely. Damn you to hell. Which reminded her...

'By the way,' she made her voice deliberately casual, 'I think my father intends to invite the new Werner Langton supremo down here from time to time. Can you keep me posted about this, please, so that I can avoid him?'

'Avoid him?' Her aunt's expression was openly startled. 'But I thought...' She paused for a moment. 'My dear, are you sure this is wise?'

Darcy raised her brows. 'Why not?'

'Because your father wants you and Mr Castille to—get on together. You know that.'

'I also know it's not going to happen,' Darcy said defiantly. 'As I've told him. I can't stand the man.'

Aunt Freddie gave her a quizzical look. 'I'd have thought most young women would find him seriously attractive,' she commented.

'You're the artist, Freddie, dear,' Darcy countered. 'You always told me to look below the surface. Perhaps I don't like what I see.'

'Really?' her aunt said drily, and paused. 'Do you still insist you never met before the other night, Darcy? Because he certainly seemed to remember you.'

Darcy shrugged. 'It's probably his mistaken notion of a chat-up line,' she evaded.

'I shouldn't think he needs one,' said Aunt Freddie, clearly hell-bent on being irritating. 'He's good-looking, successful and wealthy. The average girl would generally find that enough.'

Darcy forced a smile. 'Then I must be the exception that proves the rule,' she said lightly. 'But you will tip me off when he's expected, won't you?'

Her aunt sighed. 'If that's what you really want.' She hesitated, then said reluctantly, 'As it happens, your father telephoned just before you arrived. It seems they'll both be down tomorrow evening.'

'My God,' Darcy said slowly. 'He doesn't waste any time.' She shrugged. 'Thank you, Freddie dearest. I'll be gone in the morning.'

'And what am I to tell your father?' Aunt Freddie gave her a level look.

'That history's repeating itself, and you have another migraine, perhaps?'

There was a taut silence. Darcy bit her lip. She said in a low voice, 'I truly wish I could tell you about that, but I can't. One day, perhaps. Anyway,' she added more robustly, 'tell Dad you don't know what I'm doing. After all, I'm free, and in six months I'll be twenty-one. Do I have to explain how I'm spending my weekends?'

'You'd think not,' her aunt agreed. 'But where Gavin's concerned, the usual rules rarely apply. And I warn you now that he's going to be bitterly disappointed.'

When Darcy got back to Chelsea, Mrs Inman was clearly surprised to see her.

'Mr Langton said you'd both be away, miss, and that I could have the weekend off. I was going to visit my sister.'

'And so you can,' Darcy assured her. 'I'll hardly be here, except to sleep, and I plan to eat out as well.'

'Well, if you're quite sure…' Mrs Inman shook her head, still anxious, and departed reluctantly for her own pleasant flat in the basement.

It was good, Darcy discovered, to have the house to herself, and be able to embark on a couple of days of sheer indulgence, with no one to please but herself.

She'd expected phone calls—messages on the answering machine from Kings Whitnall demanding her presence, or at least an explanation for her absence.

But there were none. Perhaps her father was being philosophical at last, accepting that she and Joel Castille would always be oil and water.

And when Gavin finally phoned on Monday morning, there were no awkward questions.

'Are you free for lunch, Darcy?' he asked. 'Then why don't I reserve a table at Haringtons for one o'clock?'

'My favourite place,' she told him happily. 'I can't wait.'

He seemed in a good mood, she thought as she rang off, because that was definitely a peace-offering. She found herself wondering how the rest of the weekend had gone, and if Joel Castille had shown any great interest in the autumn countryside he'd been invited to admire. But she immediately dismissed it all from her mind. His interests were no concern of hers. And the falling leaves could bury him alive for all she cared.

For her lunch date, she dressed in a cream straight skirt topped by a V-necked sweater in a pale honey colour. She put gold studs in her ears, and brushed her hair into silky waves round her face. She emphasised the faint almond slant of her eyes with shadow and pencil, and touched her lips with a neutral gloss.

Neat, she told herself, her mouth twisting, but not gaudy. The way her father liked her to look.

Because if, as she suspected, they were about to have that serious talk about the future that he'd mentioned last week, it would be good to get off on the right foot.

And she would raise, yet again, the subject of her engineering training. Try and make him see that she was serious. That she wanted to make a contribution.

She arrived at the restaurant a few minutes early, to be greeted by the head waiter, all smiles, and conducted with some ceremony to one of the corner tables.

The stage was definitely set for a quiet *tête-à-tête*, she thought wryly as she asked for a white-wine spritzer. She settled back on the cushioned bench, and glanced around her. It might not be the most fashionable place in London, but the food was wonderful, so most of the tables were occupied, and the room was filled with the soft hum of conversation.

She and her father had been coming here for years. Even when she was a schoolgirl, a meal at Haringtons had invariably featured as part of every half-term treat.

And maybe it was a good omen that he'd suggested meeting her here today.

She heard a sudden stir in the room, suggesting a new arrival, and looked up with an expectant smile, which froze on her lips as she realised just who was walking towards her, accompanied by Georges, the head waiter.

'Oh, no,' she wailed under her breath. 'I don't believe it. This can't be happening to me. It—can't.'

She sat in stony silence while Joel was seated opposite her, his napkin spread on his lap, and menus and the wine list ceremoniously handed to him.

When they were left alone, she said, 'Where is my father?'

'He couldn't make it.' His smile was equable. 'I'm taking his place.'

'Not,' she said, her voice shaking, 'in this lifetime.' She reached for her bag. 'I'm going.'

'I'm aware you have a predilection for making scenes,' he said softly. 'But I hardly think you want to start one here, where you're so well-known. Not if you ever want to come back, anyway.' He allowed that to sink in for a heartbeat, the continued evenly, 'So I suggest you bite on the bullet, Miss Langton, and stay exactly where you are.'

Slowly, unwillingly, she let go of her bag. Looked at him, her enemy, elegant in his dark blue suit with the discreetly striped silk tie. Found herself noticing reluctantly the long, dark lashes that fringed the vivid blue gaze—the cool, sculpted line of the hard mouth.

She took a breath. 'Why are you doing this?'

'Because I don't have a choice. If you'd spent the weekend at Kings Whitnall, this interview could have been conducted in private. That was certainly your father's initial wish.'

'I thought he took my absence far too well,' she said bitterly. 'I should have known that he'd be planning something.' She paused. 'And what interview, precisely?'

'Maybe we should order first,' he said. 'Some discussions should be avoided on an empty stomach.'

'Then I'll have the red-pepper soup,' she said, barely glancing at the menu. 'Followed by Dover sole, and a green salad.'

Joel beckoned to a hovering waiter. 'I'll have the vegetable terrine, and the sea bass,' he added, having given her order. 'And the Chablis.' He glanced at Darcy, sitting rigidly across the table, bright spots of colour flaring in her pale cheeks. 'Also some still water, right away, please.'

'You think I might need it?' she asked sarcastically as the waiter left.

'I'm still learning your reactions,' he said. 'And this is new territory.'

'Then here's a response to be going on with.' She kept her voice low and fierce. 'I do not want to be here with you. I hoped I would never see you again. I would like you to go away now. Is that clear enough?'

'Your father's wishes are rather different,' he said. 'And he's still the boss. And this is the scenario as he sees it. I stay, and we enjoy a pleasant lunch together. Tomorrow, I get my secretary to send you flowers. At the end of the week, I call you personally and invite you to dinner. After that, I have tickets for a play you want to see.

'And on we go for three months, say, when I arrange dinner *à deux*, probably at my flat, produce a very expensive diamond ring, and ask you to be my wife.'

She stared at him. 'You're quite insane,' she said flatly. 'You must be.'

'As I said, it's your father's script, not mine. And certainly not yours.'

'No.' She bit the word.

'Then why don't we save a lot of time and wasted effort? Scrub the meaningless courtship rituals, and cut to the chase.' The blue gaze dwelt on her dispassionately. 'Your father intends you to marry me, Miss Langton. So, what's it to be? Yes—or no?'

CHAPTER FOUR

THE NOISE and movement around them faded to some unknown distance. Darcy could hear nothing but the echo of his words in her head. Could see nothing but the watchful blue eyes.

From somewhere, she found her voice. Made it work.

'No. *No.* Of course not. Obviously. You—you couldn't possibly think...'

She drew a breath. Moved her hands in a quick, angry gesture. 'My God, no.'

He nodded. 'You don't think you should give the proposition some reasoned consideration?' His tone was almost meditative.

'Reasoned?' she echoed derisively. 'I think my father, and you, must have taken leave of your collective senses.'

'Why do you say that?'

'Isn't it apparent?' She took a quick breath. 'I loathed you on sight, Mr Castille, and first impressions count with me. And, of all the women in the world, I must be the last one you'd ever seriously consider as a wife. So why don't you simply tell my father so, and put a final end to this nonsense?'

'On the other hand,' he said softly, 'why don't you tell him the grounds for your dislike of me? I'm sure he'd be fascinated.'

There was a tense silence, then Darcy said, 'Are you daring to blackmail me, Mr Castille?'

'Not at all,' he said. 'Just pointing out that your continued hostility could lead to explanations we'd both find awkward.' He paused. 'Your aunt already has her suspicions.'

'Thanks,' she said, 'to you.'

There was an enforced pause while one waiter brought the water to the table, another arrived with a wine cooler and someone else came with a basket of home-made bread.

Darcy drank some of her spritzer, hoping vainly it would ease the dryness of her mouth, or, at least, calm her whirling thoughts.

This is a bad dream, she thought. One of those waking ones that leaves you with a headache for the rest of the morning. And, presently, I shall open my eyes and find I'm still in bed in Chelsea, and if that happens I'll happily take aspirin for the next week.

But then the flurry of activity round the table ceased, and she was once again alone with her tormentor.

She put her glass down, hoping that he hadn't noticed that her hand had been shaking.

She said, 'Who thought up this sick joke?'

'It evolved. Your father's a realist, and he knows that his decision to bring me into the company hasn't met with universal favour. The board might decide it prefers another outsider. Someone less inclined to upset the status quo. But as Gavin's son-in-law, a member of the family, I'd be in a much stronger position when he finally stands down.'

He gave her a level look. 'Think about it. Your father entrusts not only his company to me, but also his precious only child. That indicates a certain amount of faith, wouldn't you say? And it might tip the balance in my favour, if it came to a showdown.'

He paused. 'And our marriage could have other positive advantages, too.'

'Really?' The query was taut. 'I'm unable to think of a single one.'

Joel drank some water. 'He was telling me at the weekend that you'd once had an idea about going to university.'

'Did he also tell you he'd made sure it didn't happen? That he warned me he'd block any application I made for a student loan—tell the banks I was a bad risk?' Her voice was bitter. 'As far as my father's concerned, all I'm fit for is to act as his hostess, on occasion. My God, he'd prefer me to have a career as a table decoration.'

His tone was laconic. 'You do it well.'

'Thank you,' she said, quivering with temper.

'In between,' he continued as if she hadn't spoken, 'you've filled your time with a series of dead-end jobs that pay peanuts. Not that it matters, because you get an allowance, approved by the board, for your services. You also have the use of the house in Chelsea.'

He rearranged his cutlery. 'But that happy state of affairs is about to end. Your father is retiring, which leaves you out of regular work, and out on a limb.'

'On the contrary.' Darcy lifted her chin coldly, 'I have every intention of getting a full-time job. Even without a degree.'

'In London?'

'Perhaps.'

He nodded meditatively. 'And where do you plan to live?'

'I'll continue to live in Chelsea. It's just as much my home as Kings Whitnall.'

'Actually, no.' His eyes met hers. 'The Chelsea house is owned officially by Werner Langton. A glamorous London *pied-à-terre* for the chairman, reflecting his status, as well as somewhere to entertain clients, especially those who dislike hotel life.'

He paused. 'Of course, that's never really mattered while your father's been managing director, and chairman. He's treated it as a second home, and allowed you to do so. I can see where the confusion has arisen.'

He smiled at her. 'But once he stands down as chairman, that will no longer apply. It will revert to being a company residence. And I don't think you can afford the rent, especially without your allowance. And I'm not sure I want a lodger, anyway.'

She sat motionless, staring at him, as their first courses arrived.

I didn't know, she thought. *I assumed it was our house. Why did my father never tell me the real situation?*

She picked up her spoon, and began to eat her soup. It was very hot, and subtly spiced, helping to dispel some of the growing chill inside her. Some, but not all.

'This terrine is delicious,' he commented, breaking the taut silence. 'Like to try some?'

Mutely, she shook her head.

He studied her with faint amusement. 'Cheer up,' he said. 'You're not going to be made to starve in the gutter. When we're married, your upkeep will become my responsibility.' He paused. 'I think you'll find me reasonably generous,' he added lightly.

She put down the spoon. She said thickly, 'You talk as if this—thing was a done deal.'

'Oh, we're a fair way from that,' he said. 'But I live in hope.'

The waiters returned to clear away their plates, and bring the next course. Darcy sat with a forced smile as her fish was removed from the bone, wine was poured and vegetables handed.

When they were left to themselves again, she said, 'Disregarding personalities, why on earth should you wish to get married at all? You seem to me to be a perennial bachelor.'

'Based, naturally, on your vast experience of men.' His tone was cutting. 'But all husbands were single once. That's how it works.'

He paused. 'I've spent a lot of my time travelling—working in the field. Now that I'm putting down roots, maybe I've begun to realise the value of a well-run home.'

'But you'll have that,' she said swiftly. 'I presume Mrs Inman is also a Werner Langton employee, who goes with the house, and, as you've already discovered, she's a treasure. You'll hardly let her go.'

'Certainly not. But I think she prefers receiving orders to acting on her own initiative. And I have little time for domestic minutiae. I need someone who knows how the household works, and what instructions to give. Who can deal with sometimes difficult and demanding people.'

Darcy lifted her eyebrows. 'Do you include yourself in that category, Mr Castille?' she asked caustically.

'Yes,' he said. 'If I don't get my own way. But I'm sure you're already accustomed to that in your family circle,' he added silkily.

'And there is another consideration,' he went on, ignoring her mutinous glare. 'Mrs Inman is a worthy soul, but I wouldn't want to look at her on the other side of my table every night.'

'And that's important,' she said, 'is it?'

'Naturally.' His voice slowed to a drawl. 'A man likes his wife to be beautiful, and you, Miss Langton, are an exceptionally lovely girl.' His gaze rested briefly on the creamy skin exposed by the neck of her sweater. 'As I'm sure you're aware.'

To her annoyance, she felt her face warm slightly. 'Flattery from you, Mr Castille, is almost an insult.'

He had the gall to grin. 'And insults from you, Miss Langton, sound exactly what they are.' He paused. 'You don't think we might find it easier to negotiate with each other if we were on first-name terms?'

'No,' she said baldly. 'There can be no negotiation. I don't want to be married. Not to you, or anyone else.'

'You prefer other women's husbands?' There was a sudden note of steel in his voice.

She lifted her chin scornfully. 'I suppose you're thinking of Harry Metcalfe again.'

'Drew Maidstone,' he said, 'also seems to be in the frame, according to your father.'

'Then he's mistaken.' *As badly wrong as you are about Harry.* 'Besides, I don't think Drew stays married long enough to count as anyone's husband.'

'He has a bad reputation, and so does that yacht of his. I don't blame your father for being concerned.'

'Heavens,' she said. 'How censorious. You, of course, have always been Sir Galahad.'

'No,' he said. 'Not even remotely.' He paused. 'So, again disregarding personalities, what are your objections to marriage?'

She drank some wine. 'You made it sound very cosy and domestic,' she said. 'But it involves other obligations, which I, frankly, have no wish to fulfil. With anyone.' *And with you least of all,* ran frantically through her head.

He gave her a measuring look. 'Isn't it a little late for you to be playing the frightened virgin?'

'It has nothing to do with being scared,' she said, examining the colour of the wine with minute attention. 'My experience of sex showed me that it was undignified, painful and messy, but mercifully over very quickly. And certainly nothing since has caused me to change my mind.'

She looked at him, defying him to laugh. But there wasn't the faintest trace of amusement in the blue eyes.

There was a silence, then he said quietly, 'I'm sorry you felt like that about it.' He paused carefully. 'However, I think you may have been unfortunate in your choice of partner.'

'A common male viewpoint, I'm sure,' Darcy said with cold derision.

'And what's the next line, I wonder? "It will be different with me, darling"?'

The firm mouth hardened. 'While you maintain that attitude, sweetheart, I doubt it would be different with anyone. But that's your choice.' He refilled her glass. 'However, there's more than one kind of marriage. If you want our arrangement to remain strictly business, that's fine with me.'

She stared at him. 'You're saying that?' Suddenly she felt bewildered. 'Yet, only a moment ago, you were telling me I was—beautiful.'

'And so you are,' he returned promptly. 'What do you want me to say? That I don't find you desirable?' He shook his head. 'That would be a lie, and we both know it. I wanted you from the first moment I saw you.'

As she gasped, he shrugged. 'But what the hell? There are plenty of desirable girls in the world, and most of them, thank God, don't seem to share your hang-ups. I won't be lonely, and you most certainly won't be jealous. It sounds like a perfect deal.'

He leaned forward. 'And there's something else. Our marriage wouldn't have to last forever. Once I'm firmly established as chairman of Werner Langton, we can think again. Even your father can't force us to find each other compatible,' he added drily.

'You want a life and an independent career,' he went on. 'Well, I can fix that for you. Go to university if your grades are good enough. Study to be an engineer, if that's your dream, and I'll support you. You won't even need a student loan.'

She stared at him. 'My father would never agree.'

'Once you were my wife,' he said, 'it would no longer be his decision.'

'First blackmail. Now bribery.' There was scorn in her voice. 'You really have no scruples, do you, Mr Castille?'

'Something Werner Langton may be glad of, if they're going

to survive through the twenty-first century,' he came back at her sharply. 'It's a hard bloody world out there, and some of the board need to wake up to that.

'And so do you. I'm offering you a working partnership, Miss Langton. Length—indefinite. Terms—to be established. Take it or leave it. You won't get a second chance.'

'You have to give me time to think…'

'You've been thinking ever since you saw me walking towards you,' he said. 'You knew exactly what I was coming for. Or did you imagine I simply wanted your delectable body?' He shook his head. 'That would have been a bonus, but even without it you're still a valuable commodity, Miss Langton.

'And I can also be of service to you. If you let me. You can forget about being a table decoration, and have a career, a life of your own. But it's marriage first. That's not a variable.'

He paused. 'Unless, of course, you've had a better offer.'

'No,' she said wearily. Her voice rang hollow in her ears. 'I haven't.'

In fact, there'd been no offers at all, but that was her own doing. No one had been allowed to get near her. And this man across the table would be no exception.

'Well?' His incisive tone cut through her reverie. 'You've worked as an au pair in the past. This time, you'll be an au pair with a wedding ring. And with a dream you can make come true at the end of it.'

She swallowed. 'You promise it's just a temporary arrangement? And when it's over, you'll keep your word about my career?'

'When it's over,' he said. 'Consider the sky your limit.'

She bit her lip. 'Well, then, I suppose, if I must, I will.'

He sat back in his chair, surveying her from under drooping lids. 'I'm glad I didn't offer my heart along with my hand,' he drawled. 'I imagine it would be feeling a little bruised by now. However.' He picked up his glass. 'To the future.'

Reluctantly, she echoed the toast and drank.

She thought, What have I done? *What have I done?*

But she knew only too well. Unbelievably, she'd agreed to marry Joel Castille.

I must be crazy, she thought. Certifiable. But Joel made it sound so reasonable, so logical. A direct way for both of us to get what we want, and then move on.

But can it really be that simple?

She looked at the food left on her plate, and put down her knife and fork.

'Wasn't the sole good?' he asked politely.

'How should I know?' she said curtly. 'I haven't tasted a mouthful.'

'That's unfortunate, when we're destined to eat a lot of meals together—lunch—dinner.' He paused. 'And—breakfast, naturally.'

Her head came up. 'And what is that supposed to mean?'

He shrugged. 'I'd hate to think your loss of appetite might become a permanent feature of our life together.'

'Understand this, Mr Castille,' she said with icy clarity. 'You and I will never have a life together. And breakfast will be one of the many things we won't be sharing.'

'Most important meal of the day, I'm told,' he said mockingly. 'You don't plan to send me off to work each morning with hot food and a kiss? Your personal contribution to British industry?'

She said through gritted teeth, 'I most certainly do not.'

His grin was unruffled. 'No, I suspect a poisoned chalice might be more in your line. But that's what marriage can sometimes be, they tell me. At least we're starting off with no illusions.' He paused. 'Shall we discuss arrangements for the wedding over dessert?'

Darcy didn't bother to hide her dismay. 'Already?' She hesitated. 'I mean, it can't be that soon, or my father will start asking questions. He's expecting a more conventional approach. You said so yourself.'

'He wants us married.' There was curtness in his tone. 'He has a result. How we achieved it is our own business, surely.' His smile was cynical. 'Or do you want me to tell him that it was love at first sight, and I swept you off your feet with my ardour?'

'Of course not,' she snapped. 'But he'll know this is a put-up job, and, as I happen to be his only child, he might just want me to be happy. Or maintain a pretence of it—for appearances' sake.'

'Well, perhaps one shouldn't judge by appearances.' He allowed the waiters to clear the table, then ordered the coffee that was all Darcy said she wanted.

He said quite gently, 'Darcy, this is a pragmatic solution. History is full of them, and your father will know that. He'll also know that I'll treat you well.'

He paused. 'I presume you wish the ceremony to be held in the church at Kings Whitnall?'

'In a crinoline and veil, with Daddy giving his innocent daughter away?' she asked ironically, and shook her head. 'As you once said, white would hardly be appropriate. And I can't be that much of a hypocrite. Make it a registry office, with a couple of witnesses.'

His mouth hardened. 'You feel that will make it somehow less binding? That could be a dangerous assumption.'

'At the moment, I don't know how I feel about anything,' she said in a low voice.

'You seemed pretty certain of your opinions when this conversation began,' he reminded her drily. 'If we can't be friends, can we establish an armed neutrality, perhaps?'

She shrugged. 'We still have to set out the terms for this arrangement. After that, maybe.'

'I'll regard that as progress,' he murmured, and then, as cups were brought to the table, and coffee was poured, 'Would you like some cognac?'

'I think the Chablis was more than enough,' she said. 'I should have stuck to water. Then I might not have agreed to this ghastly charade.'

He looked faintly amused. 'Surely what we both have to gain is worth a few hours of mutual civility a week?'

'You seem to have an answer for everything,' she said curtly. 'Try this for size. What happens if one or both of us meets someone else, after we're married?'

'Unfortunate,' he said. 'Any new relationship would have to wait for the divorce.'

'And supposing you fall madly in love?' Her tone was defiant.

'Believe me, I shall do my best not to. I hope you do the same.'

Darcy stared at him. 'But there must surely have been some-one, some time that you wanted sufficiently to marry?'

'Once, yes.' He spoke lightly, but she saw his mouth tighten. 'But she had the bad taste to be involved with someone else, and wasn't interested. End of story.'

Emma, she thought with a sense of shock. It had to be Emma. The girl who'd married Harry Metcalfe and was now carrying his child. The cousin, her father said, who'd been like Joel Castille's beloved sister. Except it had been more, much more than that, on his side at least.

'But if you can't have what you want,' he continued, 'you can either waste your life brooding on its injustice, or you can set-tle for the next best thing.'

His eyes met hers, cool, unsmiling. 'Believe me,' he said, 'we can make this work.'

Can we? she thought, feeling a bubble of sheer hysteria rise inside her. *Can we?* How is that possible, feeling as we do about each other?

He glanced at his watch, pulled a face. 'I should return to the battleground. After this, it will seem like heaven.' He paused. 'Will you have dinner with me tomorrow night so we can dis-cuss the ground rules?'

'I suppose it's necessary.'

'I'll pick you up at seven-thirty. Until then I shall count the hours,' he said mockingly, signalling for the bill. 'Do you want to stay and have some more coffee, or can I get you a cab?'

'I'll stay.' She had no real intention of doing so, but she needed him to go. She wanted to be alone. To think over what she'd done, and begin counting the cost.

'Then I'll see you later.' He paused. 'Shall we shake hands on the deal?'

Almost before Darcy knew what was happening, his fingers had closed firmly round hers. And in the next instant, he was rais-ing her hand to his lips, turning it so that his light kiss brushed her palm.

As if, she thought numbly, he was placing some kind of seal upon her. His own personal mark of ownership.

Then she was free, and he was walking away across the room.

It was only when he was completely out of sight that she realised she'd been holding her breath. She released it slowly, aware that her heart rate had quickened, and resenting it.

I—I wasn't expecting it, she defended herself swiftly. And, anyway, it didn't mean a thing. He's half-French, so maybe hand-kissing is in the genes. A reflex action on his part. Nothing to get wound up about.

She drank the rest of her cooling coffee and began to count to a hundred under her breath, not hurrying. She wanted Joel Castille safely in a taxi, and on his way back to Werner Langton, before she made her own exit. She couldn't risk another confrontation—not when she was still flurried from the last one.

She'd reached the eighties, when Georges appeared beside her with a small tray.

'Brandy, *mademoiselle*.' He set a balloon glass on the table. 'With the compliments of *monsieur*.' His brow was faintly creased. 'He says—for the shock?' he added questioningly.

'That,' Darcy said, nailing on a smile, 'is *monsieur's* little joke. *Salut.*'

She picked up the glass and, still smiling, swallowed some of its contents.

But to herself: 'Bastard,' she whispered silently. 'Complete and utter *bastard.*'

Darcy was expecting fireworks when her father came home that evening—or, at least, displeasure that his scheming had been exposed, then turned on its head like this.

But his smile was calm. 'Joel has told me the good news, my dear. I'm delighted for you both.' He hugged her, then stepped back, fixing her with a steady look. 'But a word of warning, Darcy. Don't make my mistake, and underestimate your future husband.'

She lifted her chin. 'Perhaps he's underestimated me.'

He smiled a touch grimly. 'Well, your life together promises to be interesting, I'll say that. But the pair of you aren't having everything your own way,' he added with sudden firmness. 'Like it or not, Darcy, you'll be properly married in church, so let's have no more registry office nonsense.

'And I intend to give you away.'

She bit her lip. 'As part of the package?' There was anger in her voice. 'Along with the pension rights, and stock options?'

'Now, you're being silly.' He was silent for a moment, then said more gently, 'I still remember my wedding day, Darcy, and how beautiful your mother looked as she came up the aisle towards me. You are so like her, you know. And whatever you and Joel may have hatched up between you, I want you both to have the same wonderful memories. As I know you will.'

But my recollections are different, she wanted to cry out. Because every time I see Joel Castille, I'm going to think of that night when he threw me out of Harry's party—the contempt in his face, and his hands on me. Because I still feel them, deep in my bones.

And it will remind me of the pain and misery that followed—every terrible thing that I can never forget, and which he will always be part of. All the reasons I have to hate him...

She said quietly, 'If it's really so important, Daddy, how can I possibly refuse?' And despised herself for her own weakness.

CHAPTER FIVE

'YOU'RE GETTING married?' Lois repeated incredulously. She put down her coffee mug. 'But I didn't know you were even seeing anyone.' She frowned. 'Is it someone you met on Drew Maidstone's boat?' She paused, her frown deepening. 'Hell, Darcy, promise me it isn't Drew Maidstone himself. You're not planning on being Wife Number Five, surely?'

'No, no,' Darcy made haste to assure her. 'It's nothing like that. Really.'

'Then what? I mean, this has come right out of the blue.'

Darcy forced a smile. 'And for me too.'

'Well, tell all.' Lois leaned forward expectantly. 'What's his name? And how did you meet him?'

This, thought Darcy, was the tricky bit. She said slowly, 'He's called Joel Castille, and we met some time ago.'

Lois's brow was creasing again. 'But you've never said a word about him to me and you're my best friend. You came here to ask me to be your matron of honour. I don't get it.'

Darcy drank some coffee. She'd rehearsed what she was going to say on the way over, but, faced with Lois's clear-eyed gaze across the kitchen table, she realised it didn't make much sense. And that maybe only the truth would do.

She said, 'It's a little difficult to explain.'

'Try me,' Lois invited affably.

'You see,' Darcy floundered, 'there's going to be a wedding, but—I'm not really being married.'

'You mean it's some sort of elaborate hoax?'

'Not that either.' Darcy sighed. 'Actually, it's just a business arrangement, and a temporary one at that. But with a ceremony.'

There was a silence, then Lois said with a touch of grimness, 'I think this requires something more than coffee.'

She went to the fridge, extracted a bottle of Chardonnay and opened it, pouring generous measures into two glasses.

'Now,' she said, as she sat down. 'Do I detect your father's hand in all this? Just who is Joel Castille, and why have you agreed to this ridiculous arrangement?'

Darcy took a deep breath. She said baldly, 'He's Werner Langton's new managing director, and he'll be chairman when my father stands down. Dad thinks that the transition will be easier if Mr Castille becomes his son-in-law.' She shrugged. 'He's probably right. The king abdicates, and the crown prince takes his place. It makes a certain grisly sense.'

'Not to me, it doesn't.' Lois stared at her with fascinated horror. 'Honey, this is madness. You don't even refer to the guy by his given name.'

Darcy grimaced. 'For that, I'm going to need time and practice.'

'Dear God,' Lois said faintly. 'How long did you say you'd known him?'

'I don't know him,' Darcy returned shortly. 'Nor do I want to. We're—acquainted, and that's as far as it goes.' She hesitated, then decided to put all the cards on the table. 'But we first met about two years ago.'

Lois's head lifted sharply. 'Two years?' she echoed. 'But that was when…' Her voice trailed away in uncertainty.

'Yes,' Darcy agreed quietly. 'Exactly when. In fact, Joel Castille was the one who stopped me from seeing Harry that night.'

'He's the man who thought you were a stripper, and had you thrown out?' There was a brief appalled silence, then Lois shook her head. 'I—I don't know what to say. This is absolutely unbelievable.'

'He had his reasons.' Darcy played with the stem of her glass. 'The bride's his cousin, and he was trying to protect her, it seems. Stripper or no, he recognised me as trouble.' She bit her lip. 'And, apparently, Harry confirmed this when he was tackled about it later. He claimed I'd been stalking him.'

'Rotten little bastard,' Lois said with feeling. She hesitated. 'Did you tell this Joel Castille the truth, including what happened afterwards?'

Darcy lifted her chin. 'No,' she stated with clarity. 'It's over, and it's none of his damned business, anyway. Let him think what he likes.'

'Darcy,' Lois spoke with urgency, 'it isn't that simple. You must know that.'

'But it can be,' Darcy said flatly. 'Trust me. Joel Castille only wants someone to run his home, and act as his hostess. Nothing more. Well, I can cope with that, for as long as it takes.'

'Nothing more?' Lois rolled her eyes. 'Get real, darling. Have you looked in the mirror lately? You're a beautiful girl, and you'll be sharing a roof with this guy. Are you sure he'll be content to leave it at that?'

'I know that I will.' Darcy spoke curtly. 'That's what matters.'

Lois raised her brows. 'Last year, you were my bridesmaid. You know how it works. There are things called vows. So when the groom says "With my body I thee worship", you're going to shout back "Oh, no, you won't"? Is that what you're saying?'

Darcy flushed. 'Well, I'm not planning to do it exactly that way. We're going to agree exact terms in advance. And separate bedrooms is top of my agenda.'

'Then why get married in church? In fact, why marry at all? You can do the hostess thing if you're simply on the payroll. You don't have to be his wife.'

'No,' Darcy said. 'And I shan't be. It's simply a legal arrangement.'

Lois was silent for a moment. 'What's he like? This Joel Castille. Short, fat, ugly?'

'Well—no,' Darcy conceded reluctantly.

'Middle-aged?'

'Early thirties, I suppose.'

'Tall? Attractive?'

'Some women would probably think so.'

'I'll score that as a yes,' said Lois. 'Then picture this. Your

arrangement is up and running. You give a dinner party which
goes well. You've both had a few glasses of wine. He's feeling
good about his life—and suddenly about you. And you've just
admitted he's attractive, so presumably he's not a seven-stone
weakling either. Therefore, dear friend, what are you going to
do if he decides he wants more from this marriage? And posi-
tively insists?'

'He won't,' Darcy said flatly. 'After all, I'm the girl who tried
to sabotage his favourite cousin's wedding. He doesn't like me,
and he doesn't trust me either. So, I'm safe.'

'Darcy,' Lois spoke gently. 'I remember when you came back
here that night—the state you were in. You were crying, hardly
able to speak, but when you could string a few words together,
they were all about this guy who'd insulted you. Manhandled you
even. The man you're now planning to marry.'

'I haven't forgotten anything,' Darcy said. 'And that pretty
well makes me immune from him—wouldn't you say?'

'I only know that Mick was beside himself. He'd have gone
round to that club, and sorted him out, if...'

'If I hadn't started to lose the baby, and he was suddenly
needed here instead,' Darcy supplied bleakly.

She had tried desperately to blot those memories from her
mind—the initial shock—the bewilderment and pain of her miscarriage. The way Mick, then a houseman at a big London teach-
ing hospital, had looked after her, his quiet, gentle reassurances
in odd contrast to his burly rugby player's exterior. The subse-
quent trip to hospital, using an assumed name, to check that all
was well.

And afterwards, the anguished, ongoing necessity to hide the
truth from her family. A need that still existed. A secret shared
with Mick and Lois, but no other.

'So,' Lois went on, 'if the guy's such a brute, and a bully, how
can you possibly do this?'

'Because my father wants it, Joel seems to want it and I can't
think of one good reason to refuse.' She lifted her chin. 'Besides,
I'm not marrying for life—just for a year or two, if that. His idea,
not mine.

'And when the marriage ends, I get to go to university and

train as an engineer. My former husband will pay all my expenses there as a divorce settlement, and I'll finally be free to have what I want from life.'

Lois sighed. 'And that's an engineering degree, is it? Darcy, you don't have to compensate all your life because you're not a boy.'

'I'm not,' Darcy said. 'I promise.' She looked at Lois. 'So, even if you don't approve, will you still be my matron of honour—and ask Mick to be an usher?'

Lois looked at her consideringly. 'First, swear to me that Joel Castille doesn't turn you on, even marginally.'

Darcy suddenly realised she was pressing the palm of her hand—the hand he'd kissed—hard against her jean-clad thigh. She was aware of a flicker of something, deep within her. Buried so resolutely that it barely existed.

She found herself swallowing. 'How could that ever be possible?'

The corners of Lois's mouth turned down. 'Then I accept for both of us. I feel you're going to need all the support you can get. But not a breath to Mick about Joel Castille's real identity,' she added. 'Or I can't answer for the consequences.'

Now, that, thought Darcy, is something I really can swear to.

All the same, she found herself wondering whether, in other circumstances, Lois's husband might have succeeded in his aim if he'd gone to the club that night. But, to her own surprise, she realised that she doubted it. Joel's features might not have been beaten into submission during a dozen rugby seasons like Mick's, but he still looked tough enough to give a good account of himself.

A man to take seriously, she thought. And felt herself shiver.

There was champagne waiting on ice in the drawing room, when she went downstairs that evening, and her father was wearing a look of quiet satisfaction, which faded when he observed her baggy khaki trousers and loose-fitting beige sweater.

'Is that how you dress to have dinner with your fiancé?' he asked coldly.

'Bought specially for the occasion.' Darcy did a twirl and saw his frown deepen.

'You have a wardrobe full of dresses,' he reminded her. 'Any one of them would be more appropriate.'

She shrugged gracefully. 'I'm comfortable like this.'

His mouth compressed and he turned away.

She'd lied, of course. Certainly, the last thing she wanted was to look feminine, or even remotely desirable, in front of Joel Castille. But common sense told her that merely covering herself from throat to ankle in shapeless garments was never going to make the coming confrontation any easier to bear.

As it got nearer the time, Darcy's mouth was dry, and butterflies were wheeling and diving in her stomach.

And as the mantel clock struck the half-hour, followed by the sound of the doorbell, right on cue, the knot in her chest tightened uncontrollably.

Maybe Lois was right, she thought. Perhaps she couldn't and shouldn't go through with this, whatever the practicalities of the situation, or the additional inducements. If so, now was the time to say so.

But what reason could she possibly give for this abrupt change of mind?

It was too simplistic to say merely that she disliked him. Her father would demand to know what lay behind this dislike, and that was forbidden territory. Nor dared she risk him turning to Joel Castille himself, and demanding an explanation. Because what was to prevent him telling the truth, if asked? If she rejected him, he wasn't honour bound to keep her secret. And once that was revealed, other unutterable truths might enter the equation.

She looked towards the door, her mind teeming, her face blank.

Joel Castille walked into the room, then paused for a moment, glancing across at Darcy, his faint smile quizzical as if he could guess what she was contemplating. And the silent warning in the blue eyes told her unequivocally, Don't even think about it.

Then he was moving forward to greet her father, and accept the offer of champagne with a semblance of pleasure at least. Before he turned to her.

He was more casually dressed than she'd ever seen him, his long legs encased in blue denim, topped by a roll-neck black sweater, and a black and white houndstooth checked jacket slung across his shoulders. Both sweater and jacket, she thought, were probably cashmere. The jeans would have some top-designer label.

But she'd hoped he'd be in a formal suit, so she could wrong-foot him, even marginally, by dressing down herself, but as usual he seemed to be one jump ahead of her.

As he reached her, she tensed. But he only took her hand, smiling down at her. 'New image, darling? I'm impressed.'

As she realised he was not intending to kiss her, she felt her knees almost sagging in relief.

Instead, he led her back across the room to where Gavin Langton was waiting to propose a toast.

'To happiness,' he said, raising his glass.

I can drink to that, Darcy thought. In principle, anyway. Perhaps in some distant day, I may even achieve it. But not in the foreseeable future.

Joel was still holding her hand, and she tried surreptitiously to ease her fingers from his clasp, but without success.

'I gather you're not planning to dine at the Ritz.' Gavin tried to make a joke of it, but the note of faint disapproval was apparent.

'I know quite a good bistro,' Joel said. 'I thought we'd have a quiet meal this evening so we can talk and make some plans.' He smiled at Darcy. 'Is that all right with you, my love?'

She muttered something in stiff acquiescence, and his smile widened.

'Then, as I have a cab waiting, shall we go?' He took the barely touched drink from her and set it aside.

She said a quiet goodnight to her father, flung her black pashmina round her shoulders, and followed.

Joel said, 'So, why the second thoughts?'

The bistro was busy, but its clientele consisted mainly of couples, so the conversation level was held at a contented, even intimate, hum. The wooden tables were set at sufficient distance from each other to ensure privacy, and were set with candles in pottery holders, and bowls of fresh flowers.

It was a place for lovers, Darcy thought. And, in that case, what, exactly, were they doing here?

She'd been dismayed to find herself seated next to Joel on a cushioned settle, rather than at a manageable distance, across the table. Even during the silent taxi ride, she'd found his proximity disturbing. Now he was altogether too close for comfort, his knee inches away from hers, their arms almost brushing as they examined the short handwritten menus.

She wanted to edge away, but knew that he would notice and, perhaps, draw unwanted conclusions.

She said defensively, 'I don't know what you mean.'

He sighed. 'Darcy, as an engineer you'll learn about stresses and strains. And get to recognise them, too, so don't play dumb. You're considering reneging on our agreement. Why?'

She shrugged a shoulder. 'How many reasons do you need?'

'Not many,' he said. 'But they'd need to be good. Our marriage ticks a lot of boxes.'

'Except the one marked "love".' Her voice was cool and brittle. 'Which most people seem to consider the most important.'

'I thought,' he said softly, 'you'd decided to opt for expediency rather than ecstasy.'

'Yes,' she said, 'I have. Yet, marrying someone—a comparative stranger—in a spirit of mutual dislike and contempt isn't a path I ever saw myself taking.' She drew a breath. 'And making vows in church that we don't intend to keep seems horribly wrong, somehow.'

'You're telling me you believe in the sanctity of marriage?' he enquired mockingly. 'You didn't appear to have the same regard for the vows Harry Metcalfe was about to make with my cousin.'

She felt her stomach churn in swift revulsion. She wanted to turn to him, and scream the truth. Exorcise this ghost from her past, once and for all. But he'd accepted Harry's version before. Why should he believe her now?

She said tautly, 'Perhaps I felt he didn't take them very seriously either.'

'Just as long as you know now that he's strictly out of bounds,' Joel said curtly. 'I won't have Emma's peace of mind troubled, particularly at a time like this. Understood?'

'Yes.' She controlled the shake in her voice. 'I understand perfectly.'

'As for this sudden attack of scruples,' he went on, 'you don't have to worry. I won't keep you tied to me longer than strictly necessary.'

'Forgive me if I don't find that particularly reassuring.'

'Well,' he said, 'we're here to negotiate. What assurances do you require?'

She drew an uneven breath. 'I have one, main condition. You have to accept that I will not, under any circumstances, sleep with you.' She met his gaze directly. 'Do you agree?'

He shrugged. His voice was level. 'If that's what you want. It's really not that important.' He paused. 'However, I also require your assurance that during the term of the marriage, you won't sleep with anyone else either.'

She went on staring at him. 'Agreed. But why should that matter to you?'

'It wouldn't,' he said. 'But I'm investing quite heavily in you, Darcy, and your future.' His smile was thin-lipped. 'And I'd really hate to be made a fool of over an investment.' He allowed that to sink in, then added, 'In every other way, of course, I shall expect you to behave as if the marriage was a real one, instead of a sham.'

'You mean I'm to keep my true feelings under wraps?' She traced the grain of the wooden table with a forefinger. 'Not easy.'

'Nothing less will do. Meaning that if I have reason to touch you or kiss you in public, you'll kindly remember that we're newlyweds, and passionately in love, and not flinch from me as if you'd been attacked with an electric cattle prod.'

She said with difficulty, 'My God, you don't expect much.'

'I could,' he said slowly, 'demand a great deal more. But I haven't. And surely the ultimate reward is worth the inconvenience of a little public pretence? In private, of course, you can do as you like. And you can comfort yourself with the reflection that I shall be away a great deal on company business. Our paths may hardly cross.'

He paused. 'And now shall we order some food?'

Reluctantly, she glanced back at the menu. 'I'll have the *moules marinières* to start with.'

'So will I,' he said. 'And after that, shall we share a Châteaubriand? They're intended for two people.'

'If you wish.' She stared at him. 'What is this—an exercise in togetherness?'

'Why not?' Joel countered silkily. 'God knows we need the practice.'

She could probably think of a hundred reasons, with more to follow, but it seemed pointless to voice them.

She'd agreed to marry him, and now she had to get on with that as best she could. It's a business arrangement, nothing more, she reminded herself. A short-term contract that will eventually come to its end. And at least she'd had a chance to establish the small print.

When the mussels arrived they were in one big tureen, and even a few minutes' mutual delving into the delicious white wine and shallot broth to remove the succulent contents from their shells totally scuppered any chance of maintaining an aloof distance for the rest of the evening.

It was clear that she was being treated to a crash-course in intimacy.

But then, he said he'd been here before, so he must have known how it would be when he placed the order, Darcy thought, resentment simmering quietly within her.

And for a brief, uncomfortable moment, she found she was wondering who his companion had been. And how the evening had ended...

None of my business, she told herself, firmly slamming the door on that kind of unhelpful speculation.

'Here.' Joel was proffering the largest mussel in the bowl. 'My contribution to world peace.'

'A sacrifice indeed,' she said as she discarded the empty shell. 'Or did you hope I'd say no?'

'It would have been more in character,' he agreed with faint amusement. 'But will you also make a sacrifice now, and drop this Mr Castille nonsense? I'm beginning to feel that I'm taking part in some costume drama. If I start wearing knee breeches, and taking snuff, you'll only have yourself to blame.'

Her lips twitched in spite of herself. 'Actually, I think you might do rather well.' She saw his answering grin, and checked herself, continuing more stiffly, 'But, if you insist, I'll try and remember in future to call you Joel.'

The name felt awkward on her lips, and she couldn't imagine that using it would ever become second nature to her. Better, maybe, she thought, to call him nothing at all. Distance herself that way. Somehow.

The Châteaubriand when it came was perfectly cooked, and meltingly tender, served with platters of sauté potatoes, and mixed green salad, and a superb cabernet sauvignon from Chile.

Later, however, as she regretfully put down her knife and fork, Darcy shook her head at the idea of dessert.

'Just coffee, please.'

'And cognac?'

'No, thank you.' She bit her lip. 'I hardly think there can be any more shocks in store for me.'

'Cognac,' he said, 'can be drunk for pleasure alone. Have you considered that?'

No, she returned silently, *because I don't want to think of you and any kind of pleasure in the same context.*

'As for shocks,' he went on, 'brace yourself for one more.' He took a small jeweller's box from his pocket and slid it towards her, opening the lid as he did so.

The coruscating flame from the enormous solitaire it contained almost dazzled her.

She looked at it. Swallowed. 'Is this—really necessary?'

'Absolutely essential.' His tone was sardonic. 'Aren't you supposed to calculate your lover's regard by the number of carats?'

Her lips moved. 'You are not my lover.'

'Silly me. I keep forgetting. But no one else will know that, especially with this thing on your finger.' He took the ring from its satin bed. 'I think it will reassure your father that I'm very much in earnest. Give me your hand.'

She found she was praying that it would not fit. That adjustments would be needed, and she'd be spared, even for a little while, from wearing this alien, meaningless symbol.

But no one was listening to prayers that night, it seemed, and the ring slid smoothly over her knuckle into its designated place. And stayed there, glittering in the candlelight. Ice, she thought, and fire.

There was a silence, then she said quietly, 'It's very beautiful.' She lifted her chin. 'Naturally, I'll return it to you in due course.'

'On the contrary,' he said softly, 'keep it as a souvenir.' And signalled to the waiter to bring coffee.

Did he really think she needed such a tangible reminder of his invasion of her life? she wondered in a kind of agonised bewilderment as she stared sightlessly down at the table. Didn't he realise that all she longed for was to be able to forget him utterly?

Yet, from the first moments of their disastrous meeting, everything he'd said and done seemed to have become seared ineradicably into her memory.

And instinct told her that the more time she spent with him, the worse it might get.

Fate, she thought bleakly, was playing one of its cruellest tricks on her by forcing her together with him in this way.

Yet, quite apart from the guarantee of no intimate involvement, he'd claimed they would hardly spend any time together anyway, she offered her frazzled nerves as palliative. Maybe they could even share the Chelsea house like neighbours in adjoining flats—friendly, but without encroaching on each other's territory.

He'd told her they could make it work, and somehow she had to believe that. Trust him…

Also, it wasn't a life sentence. It would end once its purpose had been served. That was what she had to keep in the forefront of her mind. Make her lodestar in this tangled maze of emotion and bitterness. Her hope for the future.

Yet, at the same moment, she found her gaze drawn almost mesmerically to the brilliant glitter of the gemstone on her left hand.

Exquisite it undoubtedly was. And a message of intent. But that was all. She would not allow it to develop any undue significance, she swore inwardly.

Because, even if a diamond was forever, marriage to Joel Castille most certainly was not. And that had to be her sole comfort in this whole terrible mess.

CHAPTER SIX

AS THE arrangements for the wedding began to take shape, Darcy got the feeling that she was standing in the path of an avalanche that was slowly gathering speed and about to overwhelm her.

She had reluctantly broken the news of her coming marriage to Aunt Freddie in the uneasy expectation of being subjected to some rigid cross-examination, but, to her surprise, her aunt had simply given her a long, considering look, then remarked, half to herself, 'Well, that certainly explains a great deal.'

Darcy, astonished, could only suppose that, with her new job looming, Aunt Freddie's mind was on other things, although she'd offered what help she could in organising the wedding, which had to be a bonus.

There were, she thought, few others in the situation.

She was making a conscious effort to avoid Joel's company, without actually seeming to do so, spending as much time as she could down at Kings Whitnall.

Not, she had to admit, that he'd made any real attempt to see her alone since the night when he'd placed that amazing solitaire ring on her finger.

No real trial of her resistance for her to endure.

When dinner had ended, he'd simply escorted her home by taxi, and wished her a pleasant goodnight. No hand-kissing, or any other sort of kissing that time, or since. In fact, there'd been none of the threatened intimacies, for the sake of appearances, when she was in his company. Or, not yet.

When they were together he was invariably civil, even verging towards being actually charming, she admitted reluctantly, but although Gavin, with somewhat ponderous tact, invariably made an excuse to leave them alone together at the end of the evening, her unwanted fiancé seemed to have as little desire to initiate any physical closeness as she herself could possibly wish.

Yet she was aware, all the same, of a faint niggle of bewilderment. He'd once spoken of desiring her, she thought. There'd been times too when he'd looked at her, and it had been there, a tangible thing between them.

But it was gone now. Totally erased, as if it had never existed. And he hadn't uttered a word of dissent, then or since, about the sanctions she'd imposed on their future relationship.

She found herself wondering if Joel ever gave her a second thought when she was not actually there, in his presence, and decided that he probably didn't. To him, this was just one more business contract among the many.

She, however, was unable to dismiss him from her own mind quite so easily. This enormous rock, for instance, was a constant reminder. It was so blatantly *there* that she couldn't avoid it, she thought bitterly.

There were times, of course, when she was obliged to return to London, usually at her father's insistence. It was during one of these visits that Lois took her to the wedding boutique where she'd hired her own bridal gown and where she forthrightly condemned the severely cut white satin suit with its tight skirt, and almost mannish lapels, that Darcy chose pretty well at random.

'It's chic,' Darcy defended.

'With a skirt you can barely walk in? You'll hobble up the aisle as if your legs have been stapled together. Which may well be the case,' she added affably. 'But do you want the world to know?'

She had a brief chat to the assistant, whereupon Darcy found herself being zipped instead into an enchantingly pretty creation in billowing wild silk and chiffon.

'If you're really hell-bent on doing this crazy thing,' Lois whispered grimly in the changing room, 'then you're going to do it properly. Look like the romantic, ethereal bride every man secretly wants.'

'Not Joel,' Darcy returned frostily. 'I don't think he does ethereal.' She turned to the bemused assistant. 'Have you anything that looks like a dam project in Sierra Leone?'

'We'll take it,' Lois put in hastily as the assistant's jaw dropped. Eyes glinting, she did a last twirl in the slim-fitting hyacinth-blue sheath she'd picked. 'And I'll have this.'

Over lunch, she fixed Darcy with a militant stare. 'So, when are you going to introduce your future husband to your friends, lady?'

Darcy bit her lip. 'I hadn't really thought about it.'

'Then start now,' Lois advised cordially. 'Mick was asking questions the other night, and I had no answers.' She paused. 'Have you met Joel's best man yet? Do you even know who he's going to be?'

Darcy probed her Caesar salad with a fork as if the contents fascinated her. 'Well—no,' she admitted.

Her friend sighed. 'Honey, if you want everyone to know there's something phoney about this wedding, then you're going exactly the right way about it.'

'Well, what do you suggest?' Darcy asked defensively. 'That we all meet up for a cosy dinner some night?'

'I feel it might help,' Lois said drily. 'Cut out all those awkward introductions at the altar rail.'

Darcy winced. 'Actually, you could be right,' she said reluctantly. 'I'll mention it to Joel. I think he'll be at the house tonight.'

'You only think?' Lois shook her head wearily. 'Darcy—that says it all.'

Darcy ate her meal quietly that evening, lending only half an ear to the business talk being briskly conducted between Joel and her father.

When dinner was over, and coffee had been taken in the drawing room, Gavin made his usual discreet withdrawal, leaving the engaged couple alone.

By this time, Darcy knew the drill. A few awkward and generally silent moments would elapse, then Joel would look at his watch, thank her for an enjoyable evening, and go.

But this time, as he got to his feet, she rose too.

'Can you spare me a few moments, please?' Her voice seemed strained, husky. 'I think we should talk.'

'That sounds ominous,' he commented lightly. 'Are you planning to tell me you've changed your mind?'

'No.' She looked down at the carpet. 'I'm still prepared to go through with it, if you are.'

'Oh, I'm all for it, naturally.' His mouth twisted. 'So how long do I allow for this unexpected encounter?'

'What do you mean?'

'Do I let my driver wait? Or tell him to come back in the morning, perhaps?'

Her startled eyes met his. 'Don't be so absurd,' she said hoarsely.

He shrugged. 'You've never wanted to be alone with me before. And I can still dream.' He re-seated himself in the corner of the sofa, stretching long legs in front of him, undoing a couple of buttons on his waistcoat as he studied her dispassionately. 'So, what have you got to say to me?'

She'd rehearsed all afternoon, but, somehow, it didn't make centre stage any easier. And his own attitude didn't help, she thought resentfully.

She took an armchair, adjacent but at a safe distance, perching on the edge of it. 'There are a number of practical details we need to discuss.'

'Such as?'

'Well, the invitations have come from the printers, but I don't know yet what names you want on the guest list.' She paused. 'Your parents, for instance. You've never mentioned them.'

'You've never asked.' His mouth twisted. 'But you need not trouble yourself. They've both been dead for several years.'

'Oh,' Darcy said, after a pause. 'Well—I'm sorry.'

'Why?' he asked. 'After all, you never knew them. However, it's a kind thought. Perhaps I should treasure it for its rarity.'

He smiled at her lightly. 'And my aunt and uncle won't be attending either. Since Uncle Peter retired they've been going on adventure holidays, and this time it's a tour of the Australian outback. And I hardly think we want to invite Emma and Harry,' he added cynically. 'As for the other guests—I'll get my secretary to send you a memo. Anything else?'

She hesitated. 'Well, I've asked my closest friend, Lois, to be my attendant, and her husband, Mick, one of the ushers. I—I don't know who your best man is going to be, but I thought maybe we should all—meet.' She paused, then added, 'At some point.'

His brows lifted. 'You thought?' he queried sardonically.

'No,' she said stonily. 'Not precisely. As a matter of fact, it was Lois's idea. She and her husband are beginning to find it strange that they've never even been introduced to you.' She swallowed. 'And your best man might feel the same. About me.'

Joel tapped a thoughtful forefinger against his teeth. 'Then, why not?' he said slowly. 'One of my old school mates, Greg Latimer, is acting for me. He's married to a girl called Maisie. I'll see how their diary stands, and come up with a few dates. Maybe you'll do the same with your friends.'

'Yes,' she said. 'OK. Fine. I don't think there's anything else. Not at this juncture anyway.'

He looked at her with faint mockery. 'You realise you may be letting yourself in for a tricky night?'

'A meal in a restaurant is pretty harmless.'

'But we'll be on show, sweetheart,' he said softly. 'Lovers supposedly in love, confronted by two other couples who've been there, and done that already. Who can remember the ex-hilaration of that headlong dash to the altar. The joy of being able to say " my husband" and "my wife".'

There was an odd note in his voice that made her heart lurch in sudden confusion. Something which scared her.

'Goodness,' she said in a voice that was sharper than she intended. 'Such unwonted eloquence.'

He sighed. 'Darcy, this will be our first public appearance to-gether as a couple, and the way things are they're going to see straight through us. That is not what I want. And certainly not what we agreed,' he added with a touch of grimness that wasn't lost on her.

She bit her lip. 'As they're all such old friends, why don't we simply come clean and tell them the truth about the marriage?' She thought guiltily, *As I've already done with Lois...*

'And why not take out full-page ads in all the tabloids too?'

he asked coldly. He shook his head. 'No, darling, we play this according to our unwritten rules. In private, I forgo the delight of sleeping in your bed, and in public, you behave as if we were passionately in love.

'And that doesn't involve sitting several feet away from me, looking like a rabbit caught in the headlights,' he added drily.

There was an odd tingling silence. Darcy felt a shiver run from the nape of her neck to the base of her spine as his gaze met hers. Held it.

Oh, God, she thought. It was happening at last. The moment of truth had arrived, and she wasn't sure how to deal with it. With him...

Joel patted the sofa beside him. 'Come here.' The invitation was spoken softly, but it brooked no refusal.

Slowly, mutinously, Darcy obeyed, occupying a space as far from him as the width of the sofa allowed.

'No,' he said. 'Closer than that, my sweet.' His smile seemed to graze her skin. 'Within kissing distance, please.'

Her whole body went rigid, then she turned on him furiously. 'You must be joking.' She almost spat the words. 'Don't even think about it.'

'Why not? It's going to happen sooner or later,' he said, his tone unforgivably casual. 'And when it does, I'd prefer you to accept the fact and not leap away from me like a frog on speed.'

'What a charming image.' She glared at him. 'There's not much anyone could teach you about romance.'

'And I,' he said, 'thought that romance was the last thing you wanted—particularly from me.' He allowed her a moment to digest that, then continued, 'On the other hand, we should be able to produce the occasional show of spurious affection. Enough to convince the world at large that we're in love, and even fool our friends and family, just as long as they don't peer too closely. Agreed?'

Her gaze faltered. Fell away to the cold glitter of his diamond on her hand, reminding her once more of its significance. Of exactly what she'd committed herself to.

She said thickly, 'I don't seem to have much of a choice.'

There was a silence, then he said, his voice quivering with

amusement, 'Tell me something, darling. Were you put on this earth for the sole purpose of crushing my self-esteem? Because you're doing a fabulous job.'

She said curtly, 'I doubt there'll be any lasting damage. Even so, it will hardly keep me awake at nights.'

'Which leaves me wondering what might,' he said softly. 'In the meantime…' He moved slightly, invitingly, stretching an arm along the cushions, and summoning her to move within its curve.

Reluctantly, Darcy complied.

There was another pause, then Joel said quite gently, 'Sweetheart, you're trembling. What on earth do you imagine I'm going to do to you?' His long fingers captured her chin. Turned her to face him. 'This is no big deal. Relax. You've been kissed before.'

Yes, she thought, the sweep of her lashes veiling her eyes as the breath caught in her throat. But not that often. And never since that night when Harry…

She realised that she was near enough to Joel now to feel the warmth of his lean body. To breathe the clean male scent of his skin commingled with the faint musk of the cologne he used.

These were the things that had emblazoned themselves on her senses two years ago when he'd first put his hands on her, she thought angrily, and, to her lasting shame, had reawoken her awareness as soon as they'd met again.

Part of the memories that she could not escape.

But at least now she did not have to look at him. Or see him looking at her.

As her eyes closed she felt Joel's lips touch her hair, her temples, and move down to her cheek, light as the tracery on a butterfly's wing, while his fingers stroked the delicate line of her jaw and throat.

Then, with equal gentleness, he kissed the corners of her inimically compressed mouth, and she felt the sharp, painful thud of her pulses as she found herself waiting…

But there was nothing to anticipate. Because Joel was straightening suddenly. Releasing her.

He said quietly, 'There. Was that really so bad?'

Her eyes flew open and she stared at him, but there was nothing to be learned from his enigmatic blue gaze.

She knew, if she was honest, that she'd admit the soft brush of his mouth on her skin had been strangely unnerving. That his forbearance had surprised her. Maybe even intrigued her a little.

Which was just as disturbing, in fact, as the knowledge that she could have drawn back at any time, and yet, for some unfathomable reason, had not done so.

However, this was not a situation for honesty, but sheer survival.

She made herself shrug. 'Rather like banging your head against a brick wall,' she said, with an assumption of coolness. 'So nice when it stops.'

His mouth twisted. 'Something tells me I'm the one banging his head against a wall,' he drawled.

'I don't know what else you expect.' There was a defensive note in her voice. 'I can't help it if I feel—nothing.'

'You mean I leave you cold?' He sounded almost politely interested. 'Then I'll just have to try harder, won't I?'

Before she could move, or protest, he reached for her again, pulling her towards him, lifting her so that she was lying across him, a virtual prisoner. Letting her know, once again, the latent power of his lean body to control—to dominate.

His hand slid into the fall of her hair, twining it round his fingers, then he bent his head and took her mouth with his, effortlessly silencing her first trembling words of outrage.

His lips were still gentle, moving slowly on hers, but the demand they created was deepening with every second. He was deliberately coaxing her to open her mouth for him, she realised. To yield up its carefully guarded secrets, then lure her further, towards the danger of a surrender as unexpected as it would be devastating. He was seeking a response.

Already a strange languor was stealing over her, the tautness and the inner trembling beginning slowly to subside, as she felt the heated silken pressure of his tongue urging her lips apart. As she experienced the beat of his heart so close to her own.

As his mouth continued to caress hers, she became aware that the pulsing of the blood in her veins was quickening relentlessly. That her breasts seemed to be swelling, the tumescent nipples grazed by the lace cups of her bra, as if reliving that long-ago brush of his fingers which still had the power to humiliate her.

And, at the same time, other bad memories were suddenly reasserting themselves too. Reminding her forcefully that she could not let this happen.

That what remained of her taut control had to be maintained at all costs.

Because she was remembering another mouth, wet and greedy, fastening itself on hers. Hands dragging and tearing at her clothing. Her own voice, scared and muffled, saying, 'Harry—no, please don't. You can't. Please don't—'

The stuffiness inside the car. The feeling that she was stifled, unable to breathe properly.

She remembered trying to struggle—to get Harry away from her, off her, and her instinct telling her that he wasn't paying any heed. That all her scared protests were going to be ignored.

And then the shock. The insult of a pain she'd never imagined as he thrust into her without tenderness or consideration.

And that was what men did, she thought as the anguish and rage came welling up in her all over again. *That* was where all the kissing led. What happened when the sweet talk finally turned sour, and they took what they wanted in any way available to them. Even by force.

She'd sworn to herself in the miserable and guilty aftermath that she would never let it happen to her again. And she had meant it. Then, and now.

Most of all now.

As Joel gathered her even closer, murmuring softly against her lips, she lifted both hands and braced them against his chest, pushing at him with near violence.

He raised his head immediately, relaxing his hold on her, his brows drawing together in a faint frown. 'What's the matter?'

She managed somehow to sound almost composed. 'I think this has gone quite far enough, that's all.'

'How strange,' he said, drily. 'I thought we'd barely got started.'

'Then you were wrong.' She freed herself completely, and moved back to the far end of the sofa, conscious of the uneven thud of her heartbeat. 'It's over. And now, if you don't mind, I'd quite like to go to bed.'

Joel's look of concern was replaced by the mocking grin that rubbed her nerve endings raw. 'Really? My ambitions hadn't got beyond the rug in front of the fire for an hour or so. But a bed would certainly be more comfortable—and convenient.'

Darcy hated the sudden heat that blazed in her face. 'That's not even remotely amusing.'

He leaned back against the cushions, the blue eyes suddenly hooded. 'No,' he said after a pause. 'I don't think it is, at that. But it's not a federal case either. So, what I ask myself is—why should one fairly muted attempt at a kiss make you so uptight?'

'A dislike of being mauled, perhaps.'

His brows rose. 'By everyone, or just me?'

'By anyone,' Darcy returned. 'But especially you.' She got to her feet.

'I'll show you out.'

Joel followed her into the hall. 'So you still felt nothing?' he asked in a tone of mild curiosity. 'Not even the slightest stirring in the blood?'

'All you aroused was my profound indifference,' she said icily. 'Goodnight, Mr Castille.'

As she reached for the heavy security lock, he came to stand beside her, his arm snaking out and drawing her towards him, while a practised hand slid under her sweater to find the still engorged peaks of her excited breasts.

His exploration only lasted one brief moment in time, but just that fleeting stroke of his fingers across her taut nipples made her body clench in a dark, shocked need she had never known before. Nor ever wanted to know. A sudden desire that she had not imagined could exist. Especially within herself.

He said softly, 'And you tell lies, Miss Langton. But what the hell, if that's really how you want to play the game? And there's no need to panic,' he added sardonically. 'Because I shan't ask again.'

He paused, allowing her to assimilate that. 'On the other hand, you can hardly blame me for trying.' His tone was almost casual. 'Willing or unwilling, you're still very beautiful. Now, sleep well, if you can.'

He opened the door, then turned on the doorstep and looked back at her, his mouth suddenly set and the blue eyes like ice chips.

'And the marriage still stands,' he told her with sudden harshness. 'So make your mind up about that. And, if kisses are taboo, start practising a few smiles instead. After all, darling, we're going to be blissfully happy.

'Aren't we?'

And he walked down to the waiting car, leaving Darcy slumped back against the wall, her legs shaking under her as she stared after him.

The marriage still stands...

His parting words continued to reverberate in her head as she closed the door, and went slowly up to her room.

Dear God, she thought, the breath catching in her throat. What have I done?

I shan't ask again.

He'd said that too, but dared she trust him after this evening? That was the question that haunted her as she undressed and got into bed.

Those careful kisses, she thought bitterly, had been planned as a prelude to enjoying a little casual sex beside the fire. He'd shamelessly admitted as much.

But, for her, sex could never be either casual or enjoyable.

Not when she was still haunted by the memory of those terrible brutal minutes with Harry and their aftermath. The events that had wrecked her innocence forever, and still clouded her life, even now.

Because they'd given Joel a hold over her. Her visit to Harry's stag party was still a secret between them, no less potent because it was never mentioned. But it was something that he could use against her if she tried to disrupt their agreement at this late stage. Even the threat would be enough.

The marriage still stands...

He'd said it, and he meant it, and she had to accept that, no matter how it might tear her apart.

She turned over, thumping the pillow, trying to find a cool

place for her burning face. And a temporary oblivion for her restive, uneasy body.

The body that Joel had so effortlessly, so cynically, aroused a few hours ago. Leaving her in a torment she was ashamed to acknowledge, even to her most secret self.

She now knew altogether more than she wanted to know about the unique masculine scent and taste of him. The way it felt to be held in his arms. The intimate touch of his hands...

And while all that might be difficult to forget, she could at least ensure that it never happened again. Prove to him that kisses were indeed taboo.

From now on he had to be kept at a serious distance, she told herself with determination. She had to rebuild the barriers between them, which had proved so ineffective just now. Rebuild and strengthen them, so that she was never again guilty of that helpless physical reaction to him, which she'd been unable either to reject or control.

Because, in spite of what had just happened, they were still strangers to each other, and that was how they would remain until the marriage ended.

When, at last, she would be free of Joel Castille. Free of him—forever.

CHAPTER SEVEN

I KNEW, THOUGHT Darcy, that an engagement party was a bad idea.

She'd just gone up to dress when her father tapped on her door to tell her that Joel's flight from Paris had been delayed, and that he was going to be late.

For a moment she felt totally blank, then she shrugged. 'It doesn't matter. And most of the guests are coming to say goodbye to Aunt Freddie anyway.'

'Well, it matters to me,' Gavin said testily, and went off to his own room.

He was looking tired, she thought, and he seemed to have lost a little weight. Maybe the hand-over of power to Joel wasn't going as smoothly as he wanted.

Another reason why she had to go along with this marriage. If she backed out, it could have repercussions all the way to Werner Langton's boardroom. Provide ammunition for all those opposed to Joel's appointment, and create problems that her father didn't need.

So perhaps her decision had been the right one, for the company, if not for herself, she thought, and sighed under her breath.

As she'd expected, her forthcoming marriage was inevitably the major talking point of the evening.

I've never been the target of so much goodwill, she thought with a slight pang of guilt as she displayed her engagement ring to another battery of admiring glances. Thank heavens, they'll never know the truth.

'And where's your fiancé?' They all wanted to know, of course, and she unfailingly replied, 'Delayed on business, I'm afraid,' even managing a note of suitable regret.

And if that didn't win her the Hypocrite of the Year award, she'd no idea what would.

But the pressure of maintaining the happy façade of the bride-to-be began to tell after a while, and she was glad to take a glass of champagne and slide unobtrusively away into the peace and quiet of the large conservatory that opened off the dining room.

It had always been one of her favourite places, its air humid, rich and raw with the scent of earth and greenery, and she breathed in deeply, pausing by the collection of miniature palms, touching the glossy fronds with a meditative forefinger.

Just a few moments, she promised herself. Then I'll go back and do my duty again.

'So this is where you're hiding. I've been looking for you.'

She'd have known that voice anywhere, and her jerky, startled movement as she turned sent some of the champagne splashing onto the tiles at her feet, and scattering droplets on the skirt of her dark green taffeta dress.

Harry Metcalfe was standing in the doorway, watching her.

She swallowed defensively. 'What the hell are you doing here?'

He shrugged. 'You once gatecrashed my party, honey. I thought I'd repay the compliment.' He watched her stiffen, and grinned. 'Only kidding. I'm staying with the parents, so I'm here, courtesy of their invitation. They cleared it with your old man first. Didn't he mention it?'

'No,' she said. 'He didn't.'

He said smoothly, 'Then it must have slipped his mind.' He paused.

'It's not really my sort of do, but I found I was extraordinarily keen to see you again.'

Her throat tightened. 'Not a view I share.'

His smile widened into malice. 'Not now, maybe, but once you couldn't get enough of me—remember?'

She felt faint nausea stir inside her, but kept her head up. 'No—I don't.'

He sighed. 'Sad how fickle women are.' He wandered across and stood in front of her, looking her over from the smooth fall of hair brushing her shoulders, down to the slender legs revealed by the brief skirt of her dress, his gaze lingering on the first soft curves of her breasts, exposed by the deep square neckline.

Darcy moved restively under his scrutiny, and his eyes narrowed a little. 'Also I gather I've been replaced in your affections by Em's cousin Joel, of all people,' he went on. 'So that makes us almost relatives, flower-face. Doesn't it?'

'Not,' she said, 'as far as I'm concerned.'

'Actually, I was convinced that Joel would stay single,' Harry went on as if she hadn't spoken. 'Carrying his torch for my wife to the grave. And, as I've always found his "Rottweiler with a bone" act a bit of a bore, I suppose I should be grateful to you for turning his thoughts in a different direction.

'Of course, Joel's devotion to Em has never involved lifelong fidelity on his part,' he added musingly. 'On the contrary, he's known as quite a connoisseur when it comes to bedtime. So your performance must have improved by several hundred per cent in the last couple of years, my pet. My congratulations.'

He gave her a long, lascivious look. 'Fancy allowing me to extend your repertoire even further before the happy day?'

Her voice was suddenly thick. 'You are revolting.'

'No,' he said. 'Just a little curious, that's all. You certainly weren't much fun when I had you before. In fact, I was surprised you went to all those lengths to seek me out again afterwards. But maybe I'd aroused your curiosity too.'

Darcy's face was ice. 'Or perhaps I wanted to let your friends know exactly what kind of a bastard you were.'

'Don't fool yourself, sweetheart,' he advised brutally. 'Most of them would have been far more interested in watching me give you some more of the same. Only dear Cousin Joel decided to play knight in shining armour instead.'

Darcy put her glass down on a ledge with extreme care. 'I'm afraid you must excuse me.' Her tone was stony. 'I need to get back to our guests. So will you let me pass, please?'

For a moment, he did not move. Then, to her surprise, he stood aside, waving her past him with a flamboyant gesture.

Darcy took one step, then another, only to find herself grabbed, his hands hard on her arms as Harry pulled her against him.

'I'm one of your guests, sweetheart,' he said thickly. 'I need some entertaining too.'

Shock immobilised her. Turned her rigid. His face seemed to swim in front of her, the grinning mouth descending towards hers. Instinctively she closed her eyes to blot him out, as bile rose acridly in her throat.

Then, above the roaring in her ears, she heard Joel's voice saying quietly, 'Good evening.'

The punishing grip was suddenly released, and she stepped quickly back, stumbling as her heel caught on a tile, her eyes turning towards the doorway, where he stood, watchful and unsmiling.

Her heart seemed to lurch suddenly.

'My dear Joel,' Harry drawled. 'I was just mentioning your capacity to intervene at exactly the wrong moment, and here you are again.' He flicked Darcy's chin with a casual finger. 'Sorry, my pet. It seems that our little reunion will have to wait for a more auspicious moment.'

'No,' Joel said, without expression. 'It will not. And don't feel constrained to stay for the rest of the party,' he added, walking slowly into the conservatory. 'I'll gladly make your excuses.'

'You mean you're throwing me out?' Harry mocked. 'I suppose it is one of your specialities, old boy.' He paused, his smile calculating. 'But all the same, there's no need to lose your cool. Just because I had her first.'

Darcy saw Joel's facial muscles tense, and his eyes go blank. Violence suddenly hung in the air like the smell of burning, so real and fierce that she almost choked on it.

'Joel, no.' Her voice cracked. 'Please don't. You mustn't...'

As the silence lengthened, Harry walked jauntily past him, and disappeared. Leaving them alone together.

'What's the matter?' Joel said at last, his voice of steel. 'Afraid I might damage that pretty face of his?'

Afraid, she echoed silently—numbly. Yes, she'd been scared out of her wits, but for a very different reason.

She lifted her chin. Met the harsh blue ice of his gaze. 'I know what you must be thinking.'

'No,' he said. 'I don't believe you do. At least I hope not.'

She swallowed, then tried again. 'But it wasn't as it looked. Really.'

'No?' he queried coldly. 'You mean you hadn't sneaked out of our supposed engagement party to be alone with him? And you weren't in his arms, with your eyes closed, waiting for him to kiss you?'

She said huskily, 'You really believe that I deliberately invited that?'

'Why not? We can hardly pretend that you and Metcalfe don't have unfinished business.' His tone was molten. 'But, apart from the fact that you're nominally engaged to me, did you conveniently forget that he has a wife—a girl worth twenty of him— who's about to give birth to their first child? Or did nothing matter to you but the passion of the moment?'

Darcy went on staring back at him, her head feeling suddenly hollow. Was it passion? she wondered. This feeling that you'd been smeared with slime? That you'd been made unclean? And that nothing would ever make it right?

Of course, she thought. That's it. To Joel, I'll always be suspect. The spoiled little tramp who chases other women's men.

It would never occur to him that Harry was going to kiss me against my will. Or that it could have destroyed me.

His only concern is ensuring there's no betrayal of the girl he loves.

The cousin who chose someone else instead of him.

It's Emma that he wants to protect, her capacity for hurt that must be shielded at all costs. Not mine. Not ever mine. Because I only cause pain. I don't feel it.

She felt a soft moan rising inside her, and bit it back.

'The saintly Emma,' she said, her tone light and hard, as she fought the unexpected, unwanted pain inside her. 'No, I certainly wouldn't forget about her.' *Or, my God, the torch you're carrying for her. Harry was so right about that at least.*

'And that's all you have to say?' he asked harshly. 'No excuse to make?'

She shrugged. 'I could say a great deal, but what's the point? And now that I've been tried and condemned all over again,' she added defiantly, 'maybe you'll allow me to rejoin our guests.'

Her heels clicked on the tiles as she headed almost blindly for the door.

'Darcy—wait.' Joel suddenly came after her. His hands were on her shoulders, turning her squarely to face him. His voice was strained. 'If you want me to understand, why not try to offer an explanation? Talk to me. I'm ready to listen.'

To other people, she thought with sudden anguish. But not to me. Your mind is made up.

She shook herself free, her face and voice cool with challenge. 'Joel, surely you must know that you're the last person I'd ever confide in about anything. Now may I get back to the party? Please?'

'Presently,' he said harshly. 'But first I think you need a reminder of exactly whose wife you're going to be. And that if you attempt to play around elsewhere while you share my name, then you'll suffer the consequences. So, sweetheart, if you're that desperate to be kissed...'

He jerked her towards him, and his mouth came down hard on hers, with none of the consideration he'd shown her before.

This time she was being punished, she realised wretchedly, and there was little she could do but stand, unmoving and unmoved, while he possessed her trembling lips, forcing them apart so that his tongue could enjoy the moist inner warmth of her mouth with a relentless pagan sensuality that was totally outside anything she'd ever experienced before.

And which scared her in a way that almost—almost bordered on excitement.

She was pinned ruthlessly against him, the heat of his hard, strong body surging through the thin taffeta of her dress as if she were naked.

Every bone, every muscle of him seemed to be imprinted on her, as if they were part of each other.

Darcy was trembling violently inside, her stomach churning and her legs turning to water. It would have been so easy in that moment to give in. To succumb to the warm weakness pervading her body, and sapping her resistance. To slip to the floor at his feet, and stay there.

But that might have seemed like an appeal for mercy, and she couldn't let him think that. There could be no quarter asked for in this battle between them.

No matter what he did, she told herself desperately, she had to maintain her stance of total indifference.

So she had to stay there, and endure. To steel herself against the calculated insult of this brutally invasive kiss that he was deliberately inflicting on her, because she could not risk making him angrier than he already was by attempting to struggle free from the imprisonment of his hands.

And as she mutely endured she found suddenly, incredibly, that she wanted very badly to weep.

And then, at last, Joel raised his head and looked down at her. A flush was staining his cheekbones, and the blue eyes had darkened stormily, almost to the colour of ink.

She heard him say something half under his breath that might have been her name.

For a moment she felt again that curious stammer in her heartbeat, as if her entire being had shifted slightly off its axis, then, summoning all her strength, she stepped backwards, shrugging off his grasp with as much contempt as she could muster.

Her breathing was still ragged, but she managed to find her voice.

'Thanks for the warning,' she said. She lifted her clenched fist, and wiped it across the new-made tenderness of her mouth, trying not to wince.

Her breasts felt crushed inside the tight taffeta that sheathed them, their rosy peaks hard and painful. There was an aching hollow inside her too, which scared her by its frank intensity.

'Now that I know what to expect,' she added, 'I'll make damned sure I don't transgress again.'

'That—might be wise.' His voice followed her, raw and husky, as she walked away from him, neither hurrying nor looking back. 'Because I have no intention of letting you go, darling, and don't you forget it.'

* * *

Darcy stood at her bedroom window, looking down at the bare garden. The sun had been shining a few hours ago when she'd come out of church, a married woman. Mrs Joel Castille.

But since then the clouds had gathered, and the view was sombre, threatening rain.

An omen, perhaps? she thought, her mouth twisting. Under the circumstances, that was entirely possible.

Lois had offered to help her change out of her bridal white, but she'd told her quietly that she'd prefer to be alone. She had not missed the anxious glance her friend had given her as she turned away.

But then she'd been well aware of Lois's concern, ever since the night of the restaurant get-together the previous week, and its aftermath.

Darcy had frankly dreaded meeting the Latimers, who were clearly among Joel's closest friends. And her nervousness was exacerbated by the fact that, since the party, contact between Joel and herself had been spasmodic, brief and formal.

And when they had met, there'd been no reference to any of the events of that evening, least of all that degrading kiss he'd forced on her.

He'd probably forgotten all about it, she thought, smouldering with resentment. But she could not. It was a constant shadow on the edge of her mind, waking and sleeping. And she found this disturbing.

As he'd driven her to the restaurant she'd sat beside him, her hands clasped tensely in her lap, wishing with all her heart that she'd ignored Lois's prompting and never suggested this.

Joel noticed, of course. 'Is something wrong?'

'I'm just wondering what your friends will be thinking about this patched-together marriage.' Darcy bit her lip. 'They must realise it's not the genuine article.'

'Not all hasty weddings are business arrangements,' Joel returned coolly. 'They might think that we met and fell so madly in love that we can't bear to wait.'

'That's hardly likely.'

'Certainly not while you're giving the impression that you expect to be hanged in the morning.'

'Oh, I'm so sorry.' She sent him a muted glare. 'You, of course, are wasted in engineering. You should have been on the stage.'

'I won't take that as a compliment,' he said drily. 'Because I'm sure that's not your intention. But years of overcoming tricky terrain, plus dealing with corrupt regimes and reluctant work-forces, has taught me to make the best of things, or at least pretend they're better than they are.' He paused. 'If all else fails tonight, try and enjoy the food.'

In other circumstances, Darcy thought, she might easily have warmed to Greg and Maisie Latimer. He was tall, fair and laid-back, while she was small, dark and cheerfully direct.

'Well, you're not what I was expecting,' she told Darcy when they found themselves alone in the powder room at one point.

Darcy carefully replaced the cap on her lipstick. 'Is that a good thing or a bad?'

'Good, I think.' The other girl considered her for a moment, then nodded. 'Yes, good absolutely.' She paused. 'You know, of course, that Joel and Emma Norton had this thing about each other?'

'It's been—mentioned.'

Maisie lowered her voice confidentially. 'The family didn't want them to marry, of course, because of the first-cousin thing. So she went off and hitched up with this other guy—Harry somebody.'

'Metcalfe,' Darcy supplied woodenly.

'That's the one. Joel had to go to their wedding, of course, and it hit him really hard. He was like a stranger for some time afterwards, and that's when he began freelancing—staying away so much.'

Her smile suddenly beamed. 'And as he's far too good to lose, thank you for bringing him back to the real world. Giving him something to live for again.'

Oh, God, thought Darcy, if you only knew. Because you and Greg are his friends, and you really love Joel, and I'm such a fraud.

She forced a smile of her own. 'I think Joel is well able to re-solve his own problems without help from anyone.'

Maisie gave her an old-fashioned look. 'Oh, I think Joel could be as vulnerable as the next man when it comes to affairs of the heart.'

Darcy hesitated as Maisie fastened her bag and turned to the door, then said in a little impulsive rush, 'Is she pretty, Joel's cousin?'

'Well, yes,' Maisie said slowly. 'In a fragile sort of way.' Then she grinned. 'Bit too needy for my taste, but I'm not a man. And the exact opposite of you, I'd say, so don't run away with the idea you're some kind of carbon-copy consolation prize. I'm sure Joel knew exactly what he was doing when he saw you.'

Yes, Darcy told herself unhappily as she followed the other girl back into the restaurant, I'm sure he did.

Joel had clearly set out to win over Lois and Mick, and, judging by the laughter from their end of the table, he was succeeding admirably. Except at one point she saw that Lois had sat back in her chair, and was frowning a little as if bewildered about something.

And at the end of the evening, when they were all departing in their separate cars, she drew Darcy to one side, keeping her voice low. 'Honey, do you really and truly know what you're doing?'

'Why do you ask?'

Lois shook her head. 'On a scale of dangerously attractive men, Joel scores lethal. And he's quite definitely someone who knows what he wants, and how to get it too.' She gave her friend a searching glance. 'You could seriously have bitten off more than you can chew.'

'Trust me,' Darcy had returned equally quietly, but more stoutly than the situation deserved. 'It will all be fine.'

Well, she had thought, she'd said it. Now all she had to do was make herself believe it.

And had turned, smiling, to say goodnight to Maisie and Greg.

Now here she was, with Joel's plain gold wedding ring on her left hand, and all the clothes for her new life packed beautifully into the elegant luggage, already taken downstairs for the journey up to the Chelsea house where she would live while her temporary marriage lasted.

Her father's remaining clothes and possessions had already been packed up and brought down to the country, while a team of painters and decorators had been installed in London to refurbish the main reception rooms. Also, she understood, the master bedroom. Which, naturally, was none of her business.

She'd examined the paint cards, along with the snippets of fabric and wallpaper she'd been sent, without the slightest interest. After all, she thought, she was only going to be the lodger. And her own room was not to be touched. She'd been quite specific about that, and received Joel's casual agreement.

Which, she supposed, was reassuring. Why, then, did she still have this vague feeling of unease?

I don't like it, she thought, her mouth twisting ruefully. It's all going too well.

There was a rap on the door, and, to her surprise, Joel walked in. He halted a few feet away from her, the dark brows lifting questioningly as he registered her, standing motionless by the window.

He'd changed out of his wedding gear too, she realised, her heart suddenly thudding, and was wearing charcoal trousers with an open-necked shirt, and a light tweed jacket slung round his shoulders.

His voice was sardonic. 'Planning to throw yourself out, my sweet?'

'Not at all,' Darcy returned coolly. 'Dad would never forgive me if I damaged his precious rose bushes.'

His mouth twisted in wry acknowledgement. 'There is that, I suppose.' He paused. 'People are waiting to say goodbye. It's time we were leaving.'

'Then we mustn't keep them waiting.' She fastened the remaining jacket buttons on her pale grey woollen suit, and picked up her gloves and bag.

Joel was looking at her wardrobe door, where her discarded wedding dress and veil still hung.

'What are you doing with those?'

'They'll be dry-cleaned, and returned to the hire company. Lois is seeing to it.'

'Ah,' he said, and there was a pause. 'No one could ever accuse you of harbouring sentimental feelings, Darcy.'

'It's served its purpose,' she returned with faint defensiveness. 'Sentiment doesn't feature.'

'All the same,' Joel said quietly, 'allow me to tell you how incredibly beautiful you looked in church today. You quite took my breath away.'

But you barely looked at me. The words hovered unspoken on her lips.

She found herself remembering how her own throat had tightened in shock when she'd caught her first glimpse of him in the formality of his morning suit, and registered all over again the stunning force of his attraction.

Yet during the ceremony he'd seemed a remote stranger, she thought, his voice quietly making the required responses, his hand cool when it became necessary to touch hers.

Thankfully, the vicar was an old-fashioned man who didn't believe in jovial enjoinders to 'kiss the bride' at the weddings he conducted, so she'd been spared that piece of awkwardness at least. Not that Joel had shown the least inclination to force any more embraces on her, she admitted.

In fact, he'd kept his distance as much as she could wish. But now, he was holding out his hand to her. 'A touch of togetherness to convince the onlookers?'

Unwillingly she complied, letting his fingers close round hers as they went along the gallery and down the stairs to the barrage of cheers and smiles awaiting them.

They were separated instantly. Darcy disappeared into a deluge of hugs from the women. She glimpsed Joel surrounded by his friends, and heard a sudden roar of laughter verging on the ribald. She could guess the nature of the joke, and felt sudden hot colour stain her face.

It was almost a relief to be out of the house and running to the car, pelted by dried rose petals.

Almost, but not quite, because she was now closed in with him in the back of his car on their way to London, and what would pass for married life. She settled herself carefully in the opposite corner, with the width of the seat between them.

So, she thought, now it begins. And found herself wondering, not for the first time, exactly what she'd taken on.

And, once again, she could find no immediate answer.

CHAPTER EIGHT

DARCY LEANED back, trying to relax, but her skirt had ridden up over her knees, and she adjusted it instinctively, her lips tightening as she realised that Joel was watching with amused interest.

'They say,' he remarked, 'that women do that not to hide their legs, but to have them noticed.'

She said coldly, 'Then what total nonsense "they" talk.'

'You sound a little fractious,' he said pleasantly. 'But that might be because you're tired. I must see to it you have an early night.'

Darcy straightened her shoulders. 'I'm perfectly all right,' she told him crisply. 'Not tired at all, so please don't concern yourself.'

'That could be a problem,' he said. 'Because a couple of hours ago, I promised to cherish you. I remember it perfectly.'

'A form of words,' Darcy said dismissively, 'which don't mean a thing.' She had an inward image of the vicar's reproachful face, and made a hasty amendment. 'At least, not to us. We should concentrate on the other promises we made some weeks ago, when this ridiculous farce began.'

There was a silence, then Joel said quietly, 'Darcy, do you intend to continue in this vein for the foreseeable future, or could we introduce a note of civility into our married life? Make some attempt to get along together?'

She didn't look at him. 'I see no problem with that.'

'I'm relieved to hear it.' There was a touch of grimness in his tone.

She turned her head, and gazed fixedly out of the window. She thought she heard him sigh, but couldn't be sure.

She bit her lip. She should be the one with regrets. And Joel had little enough to complain about. He was her nominal husband, and Gavin's legal son-in-law, which should keep the Werner Langton board quiet. And that was all that was required.

Before too long, the smooth motion of the car, the cushioned comfort of the seat and the rush of the passing landscape produced their own soporific effect, and Darcy found her eyes closing. But she wasn't going to actually sleep, she told herself drowsily. Of course she wasn't, because where Joel Castille was concerned she needed to keep her wits about her.

The next thing she knew was Joel's voice saying with faint amusement, 'Wake up, Darcy, we're nearly there.'

She sat up instantly, pushing at her hair with a defensive hand. 'I knew that, thank you.'

His brows lifted. 'Fibber,' he said softly. 'But I have to tell you that you look very lovely when you're not being tired. You even snore beautifully.'

She said between her teeth, 'I wasn't really asleep and I do not snore.'

His lips twitched. 'Of course not, sweetheart. Whatever you say.'

She sent him a fulminating look, then, still disorientated, took a belated glance out of the car window. And stiffened. Because there was no sign of the quiet Chelsea square she was expecting. On the contrary, the car seemed to be caught up in the approach to a major airport.

She turned on Joel. 'What's happening? Where are we?'

'Just coming into Heathrow.'

'Heathrow?' Darcy stared at him, her forehead puckered in bewilderment. 'Are you being dropped off here for some business trip?'

'By no means. We're here to catch a flight to the Caribbean for our honeymoon.'

She was wide awake now, and sitting upright, her heart beating like a trip hammer.

She said, 'You don't really mean that. You can't.'

'I certainly do. After the wedding ceremony, the happy couple depart for a week or two of blissful seclusion. That's the convention.'

'But this isn't a conventional marriage.' She managed to keep her voice steady.

'In some ways it will be,' he told her coolly. 'And this is one of them. I thought some relaxation in the sun might do us both good. And I think you'll like Augustina. It's a very small island belonging to a property developer I met in the States a few years back. He's built a hotel there, and scattered a dozen or so thatched bungalows through the grounds.

'The emphasis is on peace and quiet, and I'm all for that. Besides, your father thinks you've been looking pale and tense recently. He feels you need a break.'

But not like this. Never like this...

She said huskily, 'You didn't think to mention this scheme to me in advance?'

'I decided to surprise you instead,' he said silkily.

'Surprise,' she said between her teeth, 'is not the word.' She shook her head. 'I see now why I had to get a new passport in such a hurry. Business trips, Dad told me.'

'So there will be,' Joel said. His smile seemed to graze her skin. 'But for once, I thought pleasure could come before business.'

'What about my luggage?' she said, her desperation increasing. 'I've nothing suitable packed. My summer things are all in London.'

'Your father arranged for Mrs Inman to put some swimwear and leisure gear in a case for you,' he said. 'And there are shops at the hotel. You can blow my credit cards to hell and back.'

'Thank you,' she said. 'I'll look forward to it.'

But she was lying. She felt no sense of anticipation about any of it, just sick with fright.

'Our check-in's over there,' Joel told her.

'Yes,' she said. 'I—I see.'

I can't do this, she thought frantically. I have to get away.

The terminal was heaving as usual. It shouldn't be impossible to give Joel the slip, she thought, trying to calculate whether she had sufficient cash on her to pay for a cab to London. Once she got there, she could go to Lois—take cover there. Joel wouldn't follow her. She was sure of it. Because that would reveal that his bride had preferred to run out on him, rather than accompany him on their honeymoon, and his pride would never allow that.

She made herself glance around deliberately casually, then consult her watch. 'Have I got time to buy a couple of books?'

'You feel time may hang heavy on your hands?' he enquired ironically, then relented. 'Why not wait until we get to the island? They'll sell books at the hotel.'

'I have the flight to get through first,' she reminded him coolly, and saw his eyes narrow slightly. 'May I get something for you? A newspaper or a magazine?'

'No, thank you,' Joel said too courteously. 'Why not pick up a game of Scrabble or Snakes and Ladders, as well, just in case things get really boring?'

'Good thinking,' she said sweetly. 'Or even Monopoly. That takes a very long time. Never a dull moment.'

She walked off, taking care not to hurry. When she risked a glance over her shoulder, the crowds had closed in, and Joel was nowhere to be seen.

Which was just what she wanted. She looked around, trying to get her bearings—the most direct route to a taxi rank.

She was nearly at the exit, when a hand fell on her shoulder, halting her.

'Still looking for the bookshop, darling?' Joel asked pleasantly. 'I think you're going in the wrong direction. And I'd hate you to get lost.' He took her hand firmly in his. 'So let's deal with the rest of the formalities, shall we? Together? Now?'

She swallowed. 'Please,' she said hoarsely. 'Please don't make me do this.'

'I'm offering you a holiday in the sun, sweetheart,' he drawled. 'And I've no intention of going alone. And if you really need something to read on the plane, then I've brought some stuff about the island. By the time we get there you should be an expert.'

They were, of course, travelling first class, and the tall, attractive brunette who told them she was Fiona, their cabin hostess, was serving them champagne, accompanied by a red rose for Darcy.

She was smiling and professional, but Darcy intercepted the

envious look she was sent as the girl turned away to deal with other passengers. A look that shouted she knew Darcy was on honeymoon with the most attractive man on the aircraft, and frankly wished she was in her place.

Not nearly as much as I do, Darcy silently assured her.

She sipped her champagne and began to look through the information on Augustina, her heart sinking.

It certainly seemed idyllic, she thought. An environment designed for couples to enjoy romantic seclusion, and that was the last thing she wanted.

Each of the bungalows had a private swimming pool and its own plot of tropical garden, leading down to the long stretch of sandy beach.

Meals could be taken on the veranda, or up at the hotel, depending on the whim of the individual guest.

In addition, she read, there was dancing each evening, a casino, plus a golf course, and horse-riding facilities near by. What more could anyone ask? she thought ironically.

'Ever done any scuba diving?' Joel asked.

She'd been aware he was watching her. 'No, never.'

'Then Augustina could be a great place to learn. I hear the reef is spectacular.'

'Then perhaps I'll try it,' she said. 'Some time.'

One detail she'd picked up on which gave her a modicum of hope was that all the bungalows had two bedrooms, each with its own *en suite* bathroom.

Perhaps Joel intended to keep his word after all, she told herself. On the other hand, he might assume that palm trees, and surf whispering on a moonlit beach, would work some kind of magic, and only one room would be needed.

If so, he would soon find out how wrong he was. She was not in the market for seduction, however expert. And she never would be.

It was getting dark when they finally arrived, the last stage of the journey being by boat.

She was reluctantly impressed. The hotel was luxurious, but the atmosphere was laid-back, and the staff welcoming and friendly. The manager himself came out to greet them.

'Mr Castille, it's good to see you again. Mr Ferrars has had to go to Miami, but he'll be back in a day or two, and he says I'm to look after you personally, and your lovely bride.'

He turned to Darcy, and just for a moment she saw a faint flicker in his eyes, as if she wasn't what he'd been expecting. Or whom, she thought. 'Welcome to Augustina, Mrs Castille. I hope this is the first visit of many.'

She shook hands, murmuring something polite, and wondering.

A smiling man called Vince loaded them, with their luggage, onto a vehicle like an upmarket golf buggy for the short trip to their bungalow.

She said, 'I didn't realise you'd been here before.'

'I came to the opening,' he said. 'Great party.'

'Your companion enjoyed it too, I expect.' She said it before she could stop herself. My God, she thought, I actually sounded as if I was *jealous*. That I cared if he'd brought another girl here.

'She appeared to have a good time,' Joel drawled. 'We both did.' He paused. 'Do you want me to go into details?'

'No!' The denial was almost explosive.

His voice was cool. 'Then let's drop the subject.' He paused. 'And we've arrived.'

Vince helped her down from the buggy, then carried in the luggage.

Darcy made herself follow, trying not to look as if her legs were shaking under her. Because this was real seclusion. She hadn't seen another person on the way here, or even a light.

She walked through sliding glass doors, straight into a lamplit living area that occupied the full width of the bungalow, and was comfortably if simply furnished with deeply cushioned rattan chairs and sofas. In addition, she noticed, one corner was occupied by a compact but fully equipped kitchen. At the rear of the room double doors led to a passage, where Vince was waiting enquiringly.

'The bedrooms are through there,' Joel told her. 'One each side, and identical. Any preference?'

She shook her head mutely, speechless with relief, and heard him briskly directing Vince to put her case in the right-hand room, and his own in the other.

It was very warm, and the darkness outside seemed to be closing in. She'd taken off her jacket on the boat, but her blouse was sticking to her and her mouth felt dry.

Vince went past her, beaming at the money in his hand, calling a cheerful goodnight as he went. Moments later she heard the buggy wheeze into life, then fade into the distance, and knew that she and Joel were alone.

Her heels clicked on the wooden floor as she made her way to the right-hand room. Her case was standing by the range of fitted wardrobes along one wall. The wide bed was flanked by two night tables, and made up with sheets and pillows in dazzling white, with a matching coverlet neatly folded across the foot.

An electric fan turned quietly on the ceiling, and the gauzy white drapes at the tall window stirred lazily in the draught.

Apart from that—nothing. Just space, and peace.

Investigating further, Darcy discovered a frankly glamorous bathroom, tiled in white and gold, with a massive tub and separate roomy shower. The shelves above the twin wash basins held an array of expensive toiletries, and there were stacks of fluffy towels. The robe hanging behind the door was white towelling too.

No lock or bolt on the door, she registered, or on the bedroom door either. Clearly, seclusion had its limits.

Well, she was here now, and she would just have to make the best of it, she thought, unzipping her case and beginning to transfer its contents to the wardrobes and drawers.

Mrs Inman had done her proud, she realised wryly. As well as bikinis and sarongs, the housekeeper had packed several casual skirts and tops, and a couple of her favourite filmy dresses with their accompanying bags and strappy sandals.

And also, wrapped in tissue and tied with a ribbon, a nightgown, filmy as a cloud in ivory chiffon, with a bodice and straps made from tiny silk flowers, which she'd never seen before.

She was staring down at it, when she became aware she was being watched.

She turned to see Joel leaning in the doorway. He'd changed into a pair of cream denim jeans, worn low on the hips. He was barefoot, and the rest of him was tanned, muscular and bare too.

She swallowed. 'I'd be glad if you'd knock in future.'

'And I'd be equally grateful if you'd chill out,' he retorted. 'You're like a cat on hot bricks.' He paused. 'I came to see if you fancied a swim. Because the pool's right there outside the windows.'

'Thank you for telling me.' She dropped the nightdress back into her case as if it had scorched her fingers.

'Don't you like it?' he asked.

'It's—very pretty,' she said. 'I just don't know where it came from.'

'From me,' he said. 'A small gift to the bride from the groom. After all, a wedding night is a special occasion. I thought you should have something equally special to wear.'

'Thank you.' Her throat muscles felt tight. 'I—I didn't expect… I mean, I'm afraid I didn't buy anything for you.'

'That's all right,' he said. 'For the record, I always sleep naked.'

She continued not to look at him. 'I think that's too much information.' She tried to sound casual, but missed by miles. 'And no, I don't want to swim, thanks.'

'Fine,' Joel said equably. 'I'll add it to the list.'

'What list?'

'All the activities you'd prefer not to take part in.' There was faint mockery in his tone. 'Do you want to order dinner here, or go up to the hotel?'

'I'm not that hungry.'

'Well, I certainly am,' he said. 'So, why don't we just settle for tomorrow's breakfast?'

'What are you talking about?'

'The fridge in the kitchen. Sometimes people have their reasons for not wishing to be disturbed in the mornings, but still need to eat at some point. A lot of honeymoon couples stay here. Therefore there's always ham, eggs and stuff available.' He smiled at her. 'So, while I have my swim, why don't you cook me some food, like a good wife should?'

She did look at him then, startled. 'I'll see you in hell first.'

'I'd tread carefully, sweetheart,' he said softly. 'Or it could turn into a hell of your own making.' He paused. 'I'll have coffee too—strong and black. And two eggs, over easy. Sunny side up might be pushing it under the circumstances.'

He turned to go. 'And shout loudly when it's ready,' he threw back at her over his shoulder. 'When I'm alone, I tend not to wear anything in the pool either. Don't say you weren't warned.'

She watched him go, her bottom lip caught between her teeth. She had indeed been warned, she thought. Alarm bells were sounding all over the place.

She took off her suit skirt and blouse, exchanging them for a knee-length blue skirt and a matching V-necked top, both cotton. She discarded her tights too, slipping her feet into heelless leather sandals.

The idea of waiting on Joel held no appeal, but under the circumstances she couldn't afford to provoke him, she realised, heading reluctantly in the direction of the kitchen.

She filled the kettle and set it to boil, then put a large frying pan on the hob, letting it heat up before adding two thick slices of ham.

She'd fully intended allowing him to eat alone, as a kind of silent protest, but as the ham began to fry the smell made her mouth water, so she reluctantly capitulated and added an extra rasher to the pan for herself.

She put plates to warm, spooned an expensive brand of fresh coffee into the waiting cafetière, cut a bread stick into chunks, then took mats and cutlery through to the small round table in the living room.

Pride wouldn't allow her to let the food burn, whatever the temptation, so the ham was golden brown, the eggs perfectly cooked and the coffee strong and aromatic. She nodded with satisfaction, then put her head back and yelled.

He appeared promptly, his dark hair glistening, and she took the seat opposite him, stone-faced.

'This is better than terrific,' Joel commented after his first appreciative mouthful. 'Did you ever tell me you could cook?'

She kept her eyes on her plate. 'Why else do you suppose I was on Drew Maidstone's boat?'

'I thought that was open to conjecture.' His tone was dry.

'You caught me once making a fool of myself,' she said in a low voice. 'That does not make me a universal slag.'

'I caught you twice,' he said. 'But who's counting?' He

paused. 'One of these days or nights, you'll have to tell me just what you see in Metcalfe.'

'I see your cousin's husband,' Darcy said expressionlessly. 'Is that enough for you?'

'Yes,' he said. Then added, 'If it were true.'

And they finished the meal in silence.

Afterwards, Joel insisted on loading the dishwasher, a courtesy she could have happily foregone. The kitchen was too small to accommodate two people who weren't on familiar terms, she thought, and she had constantly to flatten herself against the units to avoid brushing against him. Worse, she was sure that he was quite aware of her struggles and secretly amused by them.

Once the machine was loaded, there was little to do but follow him back into the living room. She sat down on one of the sofas, feeling as if she was on a knife-edge.

There was a brief silence, then, 'It's been quite a day,' Joel said, stretching indolently, the movement emphasising the lithe toughness of his body. It occurred to her that without the formal armour of business clothes he was formidable indeed, and she felt her mouth dry suddenly. He smiled at her. 'That early night I mentioned seems like a good idea.'

'Yes.' She pantomimed a yawn. 'Perhaps you're right.' She stood up. 'There don't seem to be any keys round here. Or keyholes either. How do we lock up?'

'We don't,' he said. 'There's no crime.'

'Oh,' she said. 'Well—goodnight.'

When she reached her room she was as breathless as if she'd been running. A shower, not too warm, could be soothing, she thought, because she felt as stretched as a wire, and she really needed to sleep. Because there was tomorrow to face, and all the days and nights after that.

She used some shower gel that smelled exquisitely of carnations, and after she'd dried herself languidly on one of the enormous bath sheets she scented her skin with the matching body lotion.

Joel's gift was the only nightgown she had with her, so, reluctantly, she put it on, then went back into the bedroom.

The bed was soft, and welcomed her like a friend. She drew

the sheet up to her waist and lay staring up at the ceiling, thoughts, impressions and snatches of conversation tumbling through her mind. And achieving precisely nothing, she decided, except, maybe, to make her feel more on edge than ever.

She needed to stop thinking, turn off the lamp and go to sleep. Because things would be bound to look better in the morning.

But even as she reached for the switch, she saw her door opening silently and Joel sauntering into the room.

He was wearing a dark red silk robe that reached mid-thigh, and nothing else. 'Don't say you weren't warned,' he'd told her, and now her worst nightmare was coming true.

As he reached the side of the bed, Darcy heard her voice coming from some far distance. 'What are you doing here? Get out of my room. Get out now.'

'No chance,' he said softly. 'You're my wife, Darcy, and this is our wedding night. And I think I've waited for you quite long enough. Don't you?'

CHAPTER NINE

FOR A moment Darcy was completely still, assimilating what he'd said. Feeling the meaning invade her consciousness like tiny chips of ice. Then,

'But you promised.' The words burst out of her in a little wail of agony and betrayal. 'You said—you gave me your word you wouldn't want to sleep with me.'

'Nor will I. That's no great hardship.' His voice was still gentle. 'But I haven't come here to sleep, my lovely one. Not for some time, anyway, because I'm actually not tired at all. And neither, I suspect, are you.'

'But you let me think that you wouldn't...' Her voice rose in desperation. 'We had an agreement.'

'With all agreements, examine the small print closely.' Joel was unruffled. 'Sleeping together is such an ambiguous concept, don't you think? It can mean different things to different people. And it covers none of the very pleasurable things one can do when awake.'

He smiled down into her frightened, pleading eyes, and his voice deepened slightly. Became husky. 'And now, my sweet, I want to look at you.'

He took the edge of the sheet and turned it back, his brows lifting as he saw her nightgown.

'Almost virginal,' he remarked. 'And yet we both know that's not the case.' He paused. 'So, will you take it off, or shall I?'

She wrapped her arms round her body, staring up at him wild-eyed.

'Don't touch me. Don't you *dare* touch me. You lied to me, you bastard. You *tricked* me…'

'It's a trait we seem to share,' he drawled. 'Just be thankful we'll never have children, or heaven only knows what they'd be like.' He paused, and his voice hardened a little. 'And you weren't deceived, Darcy, whatever you may tell yourself. I told you once that I wanted you from that first moment—but you already knew that, so don't bother to deny it. It was always a question of when, so don't pretend otherwise.'

'Joel.' She was shaking, her voice sinking to an anguished whisper. 'Don't do this. I'm begging you. Don't force me. I—I couldn't bear it.'

'I don't believe in force, darling,' he said. 'Just a little gentle persuasion, perhaps. Starting with this.' He reached down and, with a deftness that appalled her, whipped her nightgown over her head and tossed it aside.

For a long moment he stood looking down at her, and she lay transfixed—her whole body burning with the knowledge that he was the first man ever to see her naked—and terrified by the open hunger in his gaze.

When he spoke, his voice was very quiet. 'You're so beautiful, Darcy. Lovelier than any of my dreams, if that's possible.'

He untied the sash of his robe and shrugged it off, revealing that it was indeed his only covering.

With a cry of outrage Darcy flung herself on her side, turning her back to him, but knowing at the same time that it was already too late. That there was another image now—unwanted but unforgettable—burning itself into her brain. And that there was nothing she could do about it.

She was aware of the slight dip in the mattress as he joined her in the big bed. She could feel the warmth of his nearness, and her stomach muscles clenched in panic.

As his hand touched her shoulder, she flinched violently. 'Don't!'

He sighed. 'I've already established my intentions,' he said. 'So save the token protests, sweetheart.'

'Don't you dare say that to me,' she whispered. 'Because I also told you something once—that I loathed sex, and never wanted it again.'

'Yes,' he said. 'I remember.'

'Then why can't you understand that? Accept it as my decision?'

'Darcy.' His voice was not unkind. 'Darling, I'm aware that a lot of girls must find their first sexual experience disappointing, but they don't take an immediate vow of chastity. Isn't that something of an overreaction?'

'I thought you were going to leave me alone.' She choked on a sudden sob. 'My God, I married you on that one condition. You know I did. But men can never believe that you don't want to be mistreated—brutalised. Because "no" really means "yes", doesn't it, Joel? Because it's what we bitches all want.'

She sat up in bed, turning on him, uncaring that her breasts were uncovered, tears running down her white face. 'That's what Harry kept saying to me all the time he was doing it, all the time I was trying to push him off, crying out for him to stop because he was hurting me so much—so badly. But he wouldn't—he didn't...'

'Darcy.' There was a note in his voice she'd never heard before—sharp, almost agonised. 'Dear God, Darcy, what the hell are you talking about? Are you telling me that Harry Metcalfe—raped you?'

'Rape?' she repeated, then shook her head. 'Oh, no, because there's no such thing as rape. Just stupid little girls who change their minds when it's too late. Didn't you know that? Harry knew it. He said so.'

Joel's face looked as if it had been carved out of stone. He said something soft and obscene under his breath, then reached over to the box of tissues on the night table and passed her a handful. Then he leaned down and retrieved his robe from the floor, wrapping it gently round her bare shoulders. Darcy clutched at it, dragging the red silk across her breasts with one hand, while she tried to mop her face with the other.

'Let me.' He took the tissues, drying her eyes and wiping her nose as if she were a child. His arm went round her, drawing her against his shoulder. 'Now tell me what happened.'

She swallowed convulsively. 'I'd been to a party at the house of a girl called Isobel, whose parents had gone away on holiday. I'd just left school, and I didn't know her very well, but I realised as soon as I got there that it was a big mistake. Harry was there, and he offered to drive me home.'

Her fingers played restlessly with the crisp edge of the sheet. 'He told you the truth when he said I'd been crazy about him for years. It started when I was thirteen, and I probably did make a hellish nuisance of myself over him. When I learned he'd got engaged, I felt as if my life had ended.

'And now here he was, being kind, offering me a lift. It was like a glimpse of paradise. But we didn't go straight home. Harry drove to Whitnall Woods, and parked there. He said he needed someone to talk to. That his engagement was a terrible mistake, and he was trying to break it off. He said he felt awful about it, because she was a wonderful girl, but not for him.

'Then he said how strange it was that sometimes the girl you really wanted was right there, under your nose, only you were too blind to see it.

'And he said, "Darcy—forgive me for being blind."' She tried to smile and failed. 'I felt as if all my dreams had come true at once.'

'Go on,' Joel directed tersely.

'He started to kiss me, and that was when everything changed. It should have been heaven, but it wasn't. I didn't like it, and I didn't know why. So I asked him to take me home, and said we could talk again the next day, if he wanted.'

She bent her head. 'He said it was far too early for that, and kissed me again. He told me I had a lovely mouth, then—then he undid his zip and tried to push my head down, towards him. But I couldn't, I just couldn't…'

'No,' Joel said quietly. 'And why should you?'

She took a breath. 'He laughed at me. Said it was the twenty-first century, and I should lighten up. That he thought blow jobs were on the curriculum of every girls' school. He squeezed my breasts, and I told him to stop, but he said he knew what I really wanted. Then he pushed me down on the seat, and ripped my underwear. I tried to scream, but everything was dark and stifling, and I couldn't make a sound. So, it—happened.'

'And afterwards?' Joel asked curtly.

Darcy shook her head. 'He said I had a lot to learn about men. That I shouldn't lead them on, then make a fuss.'

'My God.' Joel was silent for a moment. 'Who else knows about this?'

She swallowed convulsively. 'No one.'

'Why didn't you report it to the police?'

She said in a low voice, 'Because it was my word against his, and I wasn't sure anyone would believe me. He was a neighbour's son, after all, and it was an open secret how I felt about him. A big joke in the neighbourhood. I—I knew that.

'And there were plenty of people at the party who'd seen me leave with him. Anyway, he'd already established his defence. He'd have claimed I encouraged him, and afterwards reported him for revenge because he wasn't prepared to ditch Emma for me.'

She sighed. 'Besides, it also meant my father knowing, and Aunt Freddie, and I couldn't bear that. I couldn't hurt them like that, or let them find out that I'd lied about where I was going that night, because I knew they wouldn't approve. I suppose I just wanted to put it behind me. Forget what a fool I'd been—the whole thing.'

'Then why did you turn up at the club that evening? Surely not to tell him what a complete and utter bastard he was?'

'No,' she said. 'Not that. I went there because I'd just found out I was having his baby.'

There was a terrible silence, then Joel said wearily, 'Oh, my God.' His arm tightened round her, drawing her closer so that she could feel the deep beat of his heart under her cheek. 'Why, Darcy? Did you really imagine he'd help you?'

'No,' she said. 'At least—I don't know. I suppose I was totally in shock—not thinking straight. He was the father and I didn't know where else to turn. It seemed logical at the time.'

'And instead of seeing you were in deep trouble, I treated you like a tart, and pushed you into the street.' His voice was quietly bitter. 'No wonder you were so hostile when we met again. You had every possible reason.'

'Perhaps I should have been grateful.' She bit her lip. 'Later that night I had a miscarriage. I realised—afterwards—that had to be a blessing in disguise.

'I also knew, when I had a chance to think straight, that going to Harry was the very worst thing I could have done. That I'd have hated him knowing. *Hated it.* So there was something else to be thankful for.'

She turned and looked at Joel. Saw the hardness of his mouth, and the brooding expression in his eyes that spoke of anger, and something less easily recognised. Almost, she thought, a kind of anguish.

She said urgently, 'And he must never know, either. Joel, swear to me that you'll say nothing. It's over. Over and gone. And, anyway, there's Emma to consider.'

He said grimly, 'I don't think Emma's under any real illusion about the man she married. Not any more.' He paused. 'But it's hardly over, Darcy. Not with the residue of pain and fear you still have. And which I've only added to,' he added with renewed bitterness. 'Reopened a two-year-old nightmare for you.'

She said stiltedly, 'Now, perhaps, you can understand why I'd only marry you on certain terms.'

'Yes,' he said. 'It explains a great deal.'

She went on, in a rush, 'I don't know why I told you all this. I didn't intend to. I'm sorry.'

'Don't be.' Joel released his arm carefully, positioning her against the plumped-up pillows. 'After all, I pushed you into it.'

He gave her a brief smile, stroked an errant strand of hair away from her face, then threw back the sheet and left the bed.

This time she was careful not to allow even a stray glance in his direction as he walked away across the room. And when the door closed behind him, leaving her alone, she breathed what she told herself was a sigh of relief.

Yet at the same time, without the support of his shoulder under her cheek, and the firmness of his arm around her, she felt oddly bereft, although, of course, she was still wrapped in his robe.

Not that she wanted him to stay, she amended hastily. But he'd listened to her, believed her, and what was more he'd been kind, none of which she'd really expected. Especially the kindness, she thought wryly. But maybe that was just guilt.

And he was certainly the last man on earth she'd ever imagined confiding in completely. Even Lois and Mick had never known the whole truth. She'd let them think that her pregnancy was simply an awful mistake—the reckless result of too much wine at a party.

But she'd had to tell Joel, she thought with sudden defensiveness. It was the only way to deal with the threat he posed to her. To make him understand that she could not endure being taken against her will a second time. That it would be a monstrous, an unforgivable thing to do.

Which he had totally accepted.

She shivered, and hugged the red silk more closely around her. A subtle fragrance seemed to cling to its folds—a mixture of clean male skin with a hint of musk from the cologne he used. The scent of him, she realised as she breathed it into her. The essence of him, deeply and undeniably sensuous.

And that brief glimpse of him naked, however unwelcome, had told her quite unequivocally that he had a wonderful body, strong, lean and muscular.

If it had come to a physical struggle she would have lost, she thought, dry-mouthed. But, thank heaven, it had not come to that. He'd admitted defeat and gone, so she didn't have to worry any more. From now on, Joel would abide by the rules of their marriage. She was certain of it.

But even as she was still reassuring herself, the door opened and Joel came back into the bedroom. She shot up in bed with a gasp, clutching at the edges of the robe. He was wearing a towel, she saw, draped discreetly round his hips and fastened with a knot. And he was carrying a bottle of wine and two glasses.

She found her voice. 'I don't understand. I thought you'd gone. Why are you here?'

He held up the wine. 'The hotel thinks of everything, even down to the all-purpose tonic,' he said. 'I felt you could do with one.'

'I—I'm fine. I don't need anything.'

'Nonsense,' he said. 'What else do you drink on honeymoon? Of course, it's usually used to toast the successful consummation of the marriage,' he added meditatively, as he extracted the cork. 'But in our case, we have something else to celebrate.'

'What are you talking about?'

'Honesty,' he said, pouring the wine. 'You have to admit, my sweet, that it's a step forward in what we laughingly call our relationship.'

He handed her a glass, then, to her dismay, stretched himself on the bed beside her, propped up on an elbow.

She wanted to edge away, but between his weight on one side, and the tightly tucked sheet on the other, there was little room for manoeuvre.

Besides, his robe was tangled around her, and she couldn't release herself without removing it completely.

So maybe it was best to keep still, and simply play along. For the time being.

She said, with an attempt at lightness, 'Is that the toast, then? Honesty?'

'Coupled with marriage.' Joel raised his glass, watching the dancing bubbles in the lamplight. 'Whatever form it takes.'

It seemed easier to murmur something vaguely acquiescent, and drink. The wine was dry and cool against the tautness of her throat, and she welcomed the refreshment of it, sipping at it nervously until her glass was empty. Only to find Joel refilling it.

She said quickly, 'No more, please.'

'But we can't waste it,' he said, taking some more for himself. 'Besides, it will help you relax.'

'Not necessary.' She took an undignified gulp of one of the world's most expensive wines, aware that her heart was thudding wildly. 'I'm practically asleep as it is.'

'No,' Joel said gently. And the blue eyes met hers with a message even her inexperience could understand. 'No, darling, you're not. Because sleep's still a long way off—for both of us, my beautiful wife.

'And our real marriage is about to begin. Right here, and right now.'

For a moment she stared at him, her pupils dilating. Then, with a little hoarse cry she threw the rest of her champagne at him.

Joel tutted, and removed the glass from her hand. 'Such a pointless gesture, I always think,' he commented, setting both glasses on the night table. 'But there's still some left for later.'

'There'll be no later,' she said fiercely. 'I've just told you why I don't want a marriage in that sense.'

'Yes,' he said. 'I heard you.'

'Then, what part of "no" do you not understand?' Her voice bit at him.

'A bad thing happened to you, Darcy,' he said quietly. 'A terrible thing. But you can't use it as an excuse to put your life on hold forever, or deny your own sexuality. Because whatever you may tell yourself, your body's ready to love and be loved.'

'Love?' Her voice shook. 'You don't know the meaning of the word. You disgust me.'

'No,' Joel returned, unmoved. 'I don't think that's altogether true—not on past evidence, anyway. Not when I've felt your response on the brief occasions that I've kissed you—touched you.'

'Oh, God.' She wrapped her arms round her body. 'I suppose next you'll tell me I'm gagging for it.' Her scorn was withering. 'Isn't that the romantic phrase?'

He shrugged a shoulder. 'It's certainly not one of mine. Nor do I plan to hurt you, abuse you, or call you names.' He paused. 'I'm going to show you that sex can also be about pleasure. Is that really so terrible?'

'Yes.' There was a sob in her voice. 'When you know I don't want it.'

'Sweetheart, I don't think you have a clue what you do or don't want.'

His voice gentled. 'And, whatever I may have said, Darcy, I'm in no great hurry. I can wait, if I have to. But tonight, we make at least a beginning.'

His hand went to the knot at his hip. 'And now, if you still want your blushes spared, I suggest you close your eyes.'

Huddled in the robe, she glared at him. 'Alternatively, you could put the light out.'

'No thanks,' he said. 'You don't like darkness, remember? Besides, I want to be able to see your eyes, and for you to see mine.' He paused. 'And although the colour of that silk is quite incredible against your skin, you'd look even lovelier without it.' He held out his hand.

Darcy's lips parted in protest, then closed mutinously, the words unspoken. She wriggled free of the folds of silk, under cover of the sheet, and passed the robe to him. As he took it, Joel extracted a small packet from one of the pockets and put it on the night table.

She realised at once what it must be, and felt sudden heat flood her skin. It was really going to happen, she thought. He was going to have sex with her, and there was nothing she could say or do to stop him. And he was even being *practical* about it.

She turned swiftly away, burying her face in the pillow. 'You're vile,' she said in a muffled voice.

'I'm a man who wants to make love to his wife,' Joel retorted as he slid into bed beside her. 'And all the insults in the world won't make the slightest difference to that.'

When he reached for her, Darcy resisted silently, her body unyielding. But calmly, even gently, she found herself being drawn back into Joel's embrace. So she couldn't even accuse him of using force, she thought bitterly.

She lay taut and trembling in his arms, totally aware of the coolness of his skin against her own. Dreading the inevitable moment when she would find herself touched. Taken. Known completely by him.

When he might also demand that she touch him...

But, as he'd indicated, Joel seemed in no great hurry to impose his possession, as the practised warmth of his fingers began their initial contact with her skin, slowly stroking the curve of her shoulder and arm, as if he was gentling a wild creature. Just the same quiet movement, repeated over and over again, until, in spite of herself, Darcy felt the tension beginning to drain out of her, and the shaking start to quieten.

How could he? she asked herself, almost desperately. How could he do that? Why was it possible?

At the same time his lips were conducting their own delicate exploration, touching her hair, then moving to her closed eyelids, before caressing her temple, her cheekbone and drifting down to her mouth.

His kiss was light, almost questing, but her lips stayed firmly closed against him, denying him the sweeter access he sought.

She had to prove somehow that she meant what she said, she thought wildly. That she did not want him.

Joel kissed her again, his mouth moving on hers in lingering, sensuous persuasion, trying to coax a response from her.

She was suddenly aware of a strange inner tremor, like the flutter of a butterfly wing as his lips continued patiently to caress hers. A sign of weakness that she could not allow. She could not, would not risk even the slightest softening towards him, and her fists clenched, digging her nails into the palms of her hands to bolster her resistance.

At last Joel raised his head, propping himself on one elbow and surveying her, brows lifted, mouth quizzical.

'No?' he asked softly.

'No.' She stared back at him, eyes icy with resentment, wishing that her voice sounded slightly less breathless. 'I thought I'd made it clear. I'm giving you nothing.'

'Ah,' he said. 'And you think that my taking will impose some kind of hardship?' He shook his head, slowly. 'It won't, my sweet. Not on either of us, and that's a promise.'

He tossed the sheet to the foot of the bed and lifted himself lithely into a kneeling position beside her, his hands capturing her fists and uncurling them in spite of her struggles to free them. He whistled faintly when he saw the small, angry crescents in the soft flesh, slanting a glance at her mutinous face. 'Now, what caused that, I wonder?' he murmured, a note of faint amusement in his voice.

He moved her hands away from her body, clamping them firmly to the mattress on either side of her.

'Let go of me. Let go at once.' Darcy twisted furiously but unavailingly against his grip.

'Not a chance,' he said. 'But please don't stop wriggling on that account,' he added mockingly. 'You look amazingly sexy. All my fantasies coming true at last.'

She was immediately still, staring up at him, angry tears glinting on her lashes. 'This is *not funny*.' She spat the words at him.

'No,' he said, his voice suddenly husky. 'And I'm not joking.'

He bent, and put his lips very precisely against her throat, at the point where the pulse leapt crazily. Then he began, slowly and deliberately, to move downwards, allowing his mouth to explore, without apparent haste, the hollow at the base of her neck, and the slender ridge of her collarbone.

He traversed the line of each shoulder, then pressed tiny kisses on the soft inner flesh of her imprisoned arms, lingering on the delicate skin inside each elbow, before following a sensuous path down to her wrists.

Darcy closed her eyes, catching her bottom lip in her teeth, trying to ignore the strange, insidious warmth that was beginning to invade her entire body.

She felt as if she was being drawn slowly to the edge of some abyss, and that she must fight back before her mind and body went out of control, and she plunged into chaos.

He'd released her hands, so she could at least try to defend herself—attempt to push him away—but her arms seemed to have become lead weights.

He was touching her face again, stroking her cheek and feathering along the line of her jaw. Brushing the stubborn contours of her mouth with his fingertips, while his lips caressed her throat, lingered on the warm, vulnerable place beneath her ear.

She realised that her breathing was becoming ragged, and knew that he must be aware of it too.

But this, she recognised, was what had always scared her about Joel. Why she had tried so hard to distance herself from him. This desperate suspicion that he might awaken in her needs and desires she did not want to experience. That, in some strange way, she might even lose herself, and become part of him.

A suspicion that had crystallised into certainty that evening when he'd first kissed her, touched her, and during the long night which had followed, when her aching, shaken body had not allowed her to rest.

But she could not, must not, let him sap her will completely. Draw her, unresisting, into the sensuous web he was spinning round her.

Whatever he did, she had, somehow, to maintain her own integrity, to shield her against the time when this mockery of a marriage ended and he was no longer part of her life.

But even as this resolution took shape in her mind, Joel bent his head and, for the first time, she felt his mouth warm and enticing against the rounded softness of her breasts. And knew that she was right to be afraid. Because her senses were suddenly in meltdown, and the void was gaping in front of her.

She tried to say 'no' but her taut throat couldn't manage the word. Only a brief faint moan.

His hands cupped her, stroking the small, scented mounds, then lifting them again to the homage of his mouth. He captured each nipple between his lips in turn, sucking gently at the dusky rose peaks, his tongue a small flame dancing against them, teasing them until they hardened into aching, intolerable sweetness.

He could not be doing this to her, she thought from some dazed corner of her mind. Could not be inflicting this beautiful, insane cruelty on her. She must not let it go on...

But this time, when his mouth returned to hers, she surrendered helplessly to its demand, knowing that further denial was no longer possible, not when she could taste the scent of her own skin on his lips.

Joel kissed her deeply and passionately, his mastery absolute, as he explored her mouth, his tongue caressing hers with languorous expertise.

When he finally lifted his head and looked down at her, she met his gaze, her own eyes clouded in bewilderment and uncertainty.

He said her name very quietly, then slid an arm beneath her, lifting her against him so that the tips of her aroused breasts grazed his hair-roughened chest in a new and exquisite torment that made the breath sob in her throat.

Then he kissed her again, his mouth hotly demanding, carrying her away on a rising tide of sensual delight that made her burn and shiver.

His other hand was beginning to make its own leisurely journey down her body, delicately mapping each graceful curve and plane, from her ribcage to the faint concavity of her belly, even tracing with a fingertip the whorls of her navel, and measuring the slight hollow inside her hip bone.

Every touch, every slightest movement stirred her senses—made the blood in her veins quicken helplessly.

But when the stroking hand reached her slim thigh, Darcy became suddenly rigid. This was where memory returned to haunt her—remind her that ahead of her lay only pain, and confusion. A stark, physical reality that she could only recall with nausea. And which bore no relation to the beguiling sensuous caresses she'd experienced so far in Joel's arms.

Yet, as soon as he felt the tension in her body, he stopped and began to kiss her again, his tongue gently playing with hers, his fingers softly fondling her breasts, coaxing her back to trembling pliancy, and she sighed as she surrendered once more, her body sinking against his.

Somewhere, in some corner of her mind, a voice was whispering that this was what she'd feared most, this emotional subjection to him. This slow awakening of her unpractised sexuality so that he could use it against her. This was the ultimate in seduction.

His hands smoothed a new enticing path down her body, making it arch and quiver under his touch. So that this time she did not resist as he stroked her thighs apart and she experienced for the first time the sure, subtle glide of his fingers exploring her most intimate self. Evoking from her the first scalding rush of sheer physical response that she had ever known.

She cried out softly, caught between panic and shame, and Joel put his mouth to hers, murmuring soothingly.

He sought the small tight bud hidden among the moist, heated petals of her womanhood, grazing it lightly with his fingertips until she moaned in torment, with a need it was pointless to deny any longer.

Immediately the caress deepened, his fingers no longer teasing, but insistent, making her feel, deep, so deep within her, the exquisite rhythm he was creating for her.

'Oh, God.' Her voice was small and cracked. 'Oh, no—please…'

She wanted him to stop because the pleasure was almost too

great to bear, and still building, yet knowing at the same time that, if he stopped, she would die.

She could feel the hard strength of his own arousal pressing against her thighs, but, somehow, she was no longer afraid. Her body was eager, straining after the promise of completion.

As if he knew, he reached for her hand, clasping her fingers round the hotly erect shaft. His voice was a hoarse whisper. 'Take me, darling—please.'

Trembling, she did as he asked, guiding him to her, then, hesitantly, into her. Gasping as she felt him penetrate her, filling the helpless, entranced welcome of her body with one long, smooth thrust.

For a moment he was still, smoothing the damp hair back from her forehead, his eyes searching hers for signs of pain or fear. Then, slowly, he bent, and put his mouth to her panting, parted lips in a slow, voluptuous kiss.

He began to move, his pace powerful but measured at first. Driving into her, as if he were some cosmic tide, ebbing and flowing, and she the moon that drew him. And his rhythm became hers, as instinct created her response, her hands gripping his shoulders, her hips lifting towards him so that his possession was total.

His lips were on her breasts now, his tongue circling the engorged nipples, mirroring the renewed play of his fingers around her swollen, secret bud, making the breath sob frantically in her throat.

Then somewhere, suddenly, there was a tiny pulse throbbing inside her, softly at first, then deepening, the sensations intensifying until they were almost an agony. Until she was spiralling out of control, her whole body convulsing in raw spasms of incredible delight.

And as the pleasure reached its peak, she cried out in aching wonder, as if her soul was fainting.

Then, as the rapturous shuddering began slowly to diminish, Joel's own pace was quickening, his iron control splintering. Lost. His body urgent, rampant, almost tortured, as if his last moment on earth had been reached. And she heard his voice groaning in a wild pleasure bordering on savagery as he came.

CHAPTER TEN

AFTERWARDS, THERE was silence. Darcy lay still, wondering if she would ever have the strength to move again. She felt completely drained—wiped out physically and emotionally. And, suddenly, forlorn enough to feel as if she was hovering on the edge of tears.

She'd not simply come down to earth, she thought wearily. She'd hit bedrock. But what else had she really expected?

Joel moved first, lifting himself carefully away from her. He lay back against the pillows, his eyes closed and an arm thrown across his damp forehead. He was smiling, his face exultant, and she watched him, her own bleakness hanging over her like a shadow.

The conqueror, she thought angrily. With his spoils.

And with the anger came the swift, stark realisation of what an unforgivable fool she'd turned out to be.

To Joel, she'd represented a challenge. She'd told him he could not have her. She'd even told him why, confessed her terrible secret, but it had made no difference. He hadn't backed off.

It had simply made him even more determined to make her want him, she thought numbly. Although, in the end, it had gone far beyond simple need. Because he'd forced her to desire him beyond all reason or even decency. And he knew it. Triumphantly.

She could not blame him totally, of course. She could have stopped him, if she'd bitten, kicked and scratched, as she should have done. If she'd hit him—hurled 'rapist' at him too. Called him another Harry Metcalfe. Then, she would have been spared.

No, they had to share the blame. But there was also shame, which was hers alone. And she would have to live with it.

What price now her steely determination—her self-respect? she asked herself despairingly. Was there nothing she could retrieve from the wreckage? No atom of pride left to her?

'You're very quiet, Mrs Castille.' His voice was soft, almost teasing. 'What are you thinking about?'

Mrs Castille...

'Just that, if you've finished with me, I'd like you to go.' She paused then added, 'Because I want to sleep.'

'Then sleep.' He was still smiling, lying back at his ease, inviting her, she saw, to settle in the curve of his arm.

She did not move. 'I mean alone. In my own space. Or are you planning to cheat me over that as well?'

There was a silence, then Joel sat up slowly, the dark brows drawing together. 'Darling,' he said. 'You're surely not dragging us back to that ridiculous agreement. Not now. Not after...'

'Not after you made me have sex with you?' Darcy lifted her chin. 'Is that what you were going to say?'

'No,' he said, after a pause. 'It isn't. But it's an interesting turn of phrase you have there. And, incidentally, I didn't hear many protests from you, particularly in the latter stages.'

'Of course not,' she said. 'You're clearly very good at what you do, but then I'm sure you've been told that already. Many times.'

'Is this the problem?' His frown deepened. 'My alleged past?'

'There is no problem. You're my husband, as you've just signally demonstrated, and you have rights that you're prepared to enforce. And I can't fight you on that.'

She swallowed. 'But in return I'd like some of the peace and privacy you once promised me. And I'd like it now.'

'My God,' he said. 'You really mean this.'

'Why not?' Darcy said defiantly. 'You've had what you wanted. Now it's my turn. So, please go.'

'Earlier tonight,' he said, 'we drank a toast to honesty. So let's admit it, shall we?' The blue gaze bored harshly into hers. 'We *both* had what we *both* wanted, Darcy, and don't you forget it.

'So get what sleep you can, darling, *while* you can,' he added with icy emphasis. 'Because I haven't *finished* with you, as you so gracefully put it. Not by a million miles. And I want you warm, eager and wide awake the next time I invade your precious privacy.'

'I hate you.' The words jerked bitterly from her throat.

'I'm sure you do.' He put on his robe, and tied the belt. 'But eventually that won't matter, Darcy.' His voice deepened in intensity. 'Because one day, when you and I are history, you'll meet someone. A man you can love and live with. A man whose children you'll want to have.

'And, instead of cowering away from him, you'll go into his arms, joyfully and willingly, because you know how to be a woman with her man, instead of a scared child. Know how to take pleasure, as well as give it. And who knows? You might even be grateful for tonight.'

She watched him walk away across the room. Saw the door close behind him. Then turned over, and lay like a dead thing, silently fighting the acrid tears that were no longer just a threat, but a reality, burning behind her eyelids and searing her throat.

Darcy awoke next morning to birdsong, and brilliant sunlight invading every corner of the room. She lay for a moment, disorientated, then memories of the previous night came scudding back, and she gave a soft groan of dismay and disbelief. For a brief instant she glanced nervously down at the bed beside her, but it was thankfully empty.

So what could have woken her? Not just the bird, surely?

She listened, then realised she could hear Joel talking to someone not far away.

She scrambled out of bed and used the bathroom, then wrapped herself in the towelling robe, fastening its sash securely.

She padded over to the windows and pushed them open, stepping out onto marble flags, with the vivid turquoise of the pool beyond. There were loungers waiting, and chairs round a white wrought-iron table shaded by a vivid sun umbrella.

And there was Joel, dressed in faded khaki shorts that clung as if they loved him, pacing up and down, speaking into a cordless phone, his voice gentle. 'I know,' he was saying. 'I know, darling. I understand, but don't do anything hasty.' As he swung round he saw Darcy and halted, his attention totally arrested. He said, 'I have to go,' and rang off.

'Good morning.' He looked her over slowly and thoroughly, and to her shame she felt herself beginning to blush. His brows rose. 'Feeling the cold?'

'I didn't pack for myself. Mrs Inman forgot to put in a dressing gown.'

His mouth twisted. 'She's probably a romantic at heart, and thought it would be surplus to requirements.'

Her blush deepened, and she looked instead at the phone he was still holding. Thought of the snatch of conversation she'd just heard. Who was 'darling' and what did Joel understand? she wondered.

It was none of her business, but all the same she found herself asking lightly, 'Problems?'

'Nothing I can't handle.' He indicated a tray on the table, set with the cafetière and cups. 'Hot coffee?'

'Wonderful,' she said. She came forward, and seated herself under the umbrella. 'But I thought I was the domestic slave round here.'

He grinned. 'After last night, I have a different sort of slavery in mind.'

Her heart lurched, and she felt her body clench, deep inside her. *I don't need this*, she thought, with desperation. *I don't need to remember that I made an utter fool of myself. And I don't want to feel like this in the full light of day, either. That if he put out his hand and touched me, I would go up in flames…*

She put the cafetière down on the table. Kept her voice even. 'Has anyone ever told you that you're a complete and utter bastard?'

'Hundreds,' he said, unmoved. 'Bordering on thousands.' He sat down opposite, and began to pour the coffee himself. 'But it's not actually true. My parents were married, and very happily too. Love at first sight.'

'And never a cross word, no doubt,' she commented scornfully.

'Oh, there were fireworks.' He took a meditative sip. 'They were two strong individuals, meeting across the great Anglo-French divide. But the rows never lasted, and I suspect the making-up was terrific.'

'If you grew up in such a marvellous marriage,' she said, 'how could you possibly decide to settle for this travesty?'

'Because even this has its compensations,' he said softly, the blue eyes glinting with amusement, and something rather more disturbing. 'Besides, it's not going to last forever. So there'll still be time.'

'For what?' Her throat felt suddenly tight. 'I thought the girl you wanted was already spoken for.'

He shrugged a bare shoulder, and muscle rippled. 'There might be others.'

There would always be others, she thought, with a pang. She kept her voice mocking. 'Find a nice girl, settle down? Can't visualise it, really. Don't see you as a one-woman man.'

'You're probably right.' He looked her over. 'Now you tell me something. What on earth are you trying to hide that I didn't enjoy last night?'

'I'm sorry,' she said, 'but I don't have your casual approach to nudity.'

'I'm sorry too.' He was grinning again, wickedly. Inviting her to smile back, she realised. To soften. Become once more the girl in his arms the previous night.

After a moment, he added quietly, 'But surely you have a swimsuit of some kind.'

'Of course,' she admitted stiffly.

'Then go and change. It's cold in England, Darcy. Here we have sunlight and a pool. Let's enjoy them, because it could be a long winter.' He paused. 'I've ordered Caesar salad for lunch, and reserved a table for dinner. Is that all right with you?'

She picked up her coffee and rose. 'What do you care? As you demonstrated last night, you'll do exactly as you wish. Excuse me.'

She walked back to her room, half expecting him to follow. Wondering if he would, and how she would react if so. Yet not hoping. Definitely not hoping.

But she reached the glass doors alone, and when she paused

to look back he was on the phone again. Not even glancing in her direction.

She filled the tub in her bathroom, tossed away the robe and sank down into the warm water.

There were things she needed to come to terms with, sooner rather than later.

Primarily, that she was now Mrs Joel Castille, in every sense of the word, and she'd woken that morning with her body aching a little in the aftermath. Nothing too severe, even mildly pleasurable if she was honest, but a reminder of his possession that she could well do without.

She almost expected to see his finger marks on her skin, she thought, looking down at herself, but there were no obvious bruises. At least none that showed.

But then Joel was an experienced and exciting lover, who knew exactly what was needed to bring the girl in his arms to climax. Any girl, probably. Including the one he'd brought to the hotel opening. His male pride would demand it.

So there was nothing special about her, apart from the fact that she hadn't wanted to marry him, and didn't want him in her bed once they were married. And he'd set out to prove her wrong.

But then she hadn't been a real challenge at all. In Joel's eyes, she'd been a pushover from the first, and nothing she'd said, not even her pathetic, stumbling confession about Harry Metcalfe, had made him doubt that for a moment.

And it was, indeed, far too late to be coy about being naked in front of him, or even half-dressed. He was right about that, she thought bitterly.

But if a suit of armour had been handy, she'd still have tried to get into it, in spite of the heat.

She picked up the soap and began to lather herself, wondering again who had been on the other end of the phone. And whether he'd resumed the interrupted call after she'd come indoors. And, most of all, why she should find it even the slightest bit disturbing.

After all, Joel was his own man, a law unto himself. He didn't have to justify himself over what he did. And she would have to learn to keep her distance while he was speaking privately on the telephone, in case, one day, she heard something that might destroy her.

And her face crumpled suddenly like that of a child needing comfort, but knowing that there was none.

It was one of the worst days of her life, yet it should have been wonderful. This was how the guests on Drew Maidstone's boat had lived, she thought, while she was cleaning their cabins and working in the hot galley.

They lay on cushioned sunbeds, sipping iced drinks and protecting their skins with high-factor lotions. At times, they cooled off with a dip in the pool. And at the appointed hour, their lunch was served.

In this case, the best Caesar salad she'd ever tasted, brought in a chilled box by the cheerful Vince, and followed by a platter of tropical fruits.

'Mangoes,' she said, fighting a losing battle, 'are tricky.'

'Try wearing a wetsuit next time,' Joel advised lazily. His eyes went to a trickle of sticky juice making its way into the valley between her breasts, and he leaned across the table, capturing it with his forefinger then licking it off with slow enjoyment. 'Alternatively,' he added meditatively, 'just get more mangoes.'

His touch was light but it pierced her. She felt it in her heart's core, deep in her bones. A shaft of yearning so intense that she almost cried out.

Don't let him see. Don't let him know the power he could have over you. Keep it light. Don't react like an affronted nun, or he'll wonder.

She made herself smile. 'A wetsuit might be safer.'

'You wouldn't consider living dangerously?' For a moment his voice caressed her.

She shook her head, her face warming. 'I don't think so. I'm seriously for the quiet life.'

There was a silence, then he shrugged. Suddenly became brisk. 'Then you might have to rethink engineering as a career. You can end up in some very dodgy locations, and the natives aren't always friendly.'

She looked back at him coolly. 'For that, I'm prepared to take my chances.' She dried her fingers on her napkin. 'Would you like coffee?'

He sat back in his chair, watching her under drooping eye-lids. 'When you go into full hostess mode, my sweet,' he drawled, 'I feel I'm the one living on the edge. But coffee would be perfect.' He added, 'I have some work to do, so I'll have it here.'

By the time the coffee was ready, the table had been cleared and Joel was sitting in front of a laptop computer. When she put the cup beside him he thanked her almost absently, his attention concentrated on the screen before him.

I think, she told herself as she went to her room to wash away the lingering effects of the mango, that I've just been compart-mentalised. My window has temporarily closed.

She put on a fresh bikini and rinsed the fruit juice from the one she'd been wearing, taking it outside with her. It would soon dry in the sun, she thought, draping it over the end of her lounger before stretching out again, face down, sighing a little as she nes-tled into the cushions.

The meal she'd just eaten and her lack of sleep from the night before were combining to make her drowsy, and what point was there in fighting to remain awake?

Joel was working, and she—well, she probably needed all the rest she could get. And on that thought she closed her eyes, and allowed herself to drift away.

She dreamed, of course. Slow, dissolving, amorphous images that gave more pain than pleasure. Tall green gardens like jun-gles, where she walked alone. Empty rooms opening endlessly into each other. A veiled woman walking ahead of her along a beach. And a man, his face in shadow, his hands reaching for her as if she was prey.

As he touched her, as she felt his fingers on her skin, she cried out and sat up, to find Joel bending over her, blotting out the sun. Realising in the same instant that her bikini top was undone, and falling away from her breasts.

She snatched at it, holding it defensively against her. 'What are you doing?' Her voice was breathless.

'Putting some oil on your back.' He showed her the bottle, his brows lifting in surprise. 'And, I thought, preventing you getting a strap mark. Nothing else. Or not at the moment, anyway. So stop panicking, for heaven's sake.'

'Is it any wonder?' Her voice was ragged. 'Is it my fault if I'm scared to have you near me—touching me—after last night? Is it?'

He looked at her for a long moment. When he spoke, his voice was quiet. 'If that's true, Darcy, then the blame is mine, and mine alone.'

He put the sun oil on the table and walked away, disappearing back into the house. And she watched him go, her arms wrapped round her body, as if she suddenly needed to dam back some unspeakable pain.

She'd overreacted totally, Darcy told herself, caught between reality and the ache of those lonely dreams. She knew it, and now he ought to know it too, hear it from her own lips.

So she should go to him, admit to him that her stumbling words had not been true. That it was not him that she feared, but herself. Because last night she had learned things about pleasure, and her capacity for response, that had shocked her. Discovered moments when she'd ceased to function as a rational being altogether. When she'd become pure sensation.

And that just the brush of his hand would be enough to destroy her control, and make it happen again.

She had to tell him these things, and tell him now, before her courage failed her, and it was too late.

She left her bikini top on the lounger, and went into the bungalow. But the living room was deserted, and the laptop was lying closed on the table.

She tried his bedroom, tapping on the door, then knocking more loudly, before looking inside, but he wasn't there either.

Darcy went to her own room and grabbed a sarong, knotting it above her bare breasts. He must have gone to the beach, she thought, and it couldn't be far because she'd been aware of the murmur of the sea ever since they'd arrived.

She crossed the veranda, and started across the closely cropped lawns towards the palm trees that fringed them. The beach beyond was white coral, and the sea that broke on it was azure, tipped with silver foam. Joel was two hundred yards away, a dark figure standing at the edge, motionless, looking towards the horizon.

She made herself walk towards him, and he turned and watched her approach, but without coming to meet her as she'd hoped.

She halted a few feet away. 'I didn't know where you'd gone.'

'I thought I'd walk. Do some thinking.' His voice gave nothing away. It was calm, almost expressionless.

'And did you come to any conclusions?'

Say that last night changed everything. That you've realised you need me, and you want us to start again. That you want us to have a real marriage. Please, Joel, say it and mean it...

'Why, yes,' he said, in the same level tone. 'I concluded that I'd treated you with a brutal selfishness that's almost beyond belief, even for someone with my own questionable standards.'

The heat on the beach was baking, but his brief smile was ice. 'And I had not one atom of moral ground to excuse what I did, in spite of my fine words when we parted. I took you because I wanted you. It was that simple, and that bloody unfair.

'But it ends now. Because our lives are going to follow very different paths, Darcy, and that's all that matters. All that can be allowed to matter. I forgot that for a while, and I'm sorry.'

He looked around him. 'Bringing you here was a bad mistake. I thought, well, you know what I thought, only too well. Maybe we should cut our stay short. Go on somewhere else, to a bigger resort maybe. Even separate hotels.'

Now, if ever, was the moment to go to him, slide her arms round him, and say, But that's not what I want.

Except that he might step back.

'I wanted you,' he'd said. Past tense. Roughly translated as, been there, done that. So thanks, but no thanks.

Was that the real message? Telling her not to read too much into one sexual encounter, because she had no place in his future? That with him there was no permanency, or commitment, at least not for her, and that one day—one night—she would reach for him, and find him gone?

I have to be the one to step back, she thought with swift anguish.

While I still have the chance, and the will. Before I sacrifice every scrap of pride I possess, and fall on my knees to beg him for what he can't give.

She made herself shrug. 'It's beautiful here. It seems silly to leave, when we can simply agree to move on. Right?'

His nod was reluctant, but she hurried on, conjuring a smile from somewhere. 'Does dinner at the hotel tonight warrant a dress and all the bling I can muster?'

His answering smile did not reach his eyes. 'Go for it,' he said. 'I'll see you later.'

And I shall see you, Darcy thought as she turned away. See you everywhere I go, and in everything I do for the rest of my life.

CHAPTER ELEVEN

THE DRESS was a favourite. A silky, silver-green fabric cleverly cut on the bias, so that her body moved inside it like a willow in the wind. In addition, it had a seriously low neck, shoestring straps and a skirt just to the knee. Her sandals were high-heeled, and her newly washed hair curved softly to her shoulders.

She was light on the jewellery front, however. Apart from her rings, she had silver studs in her ears, and a bracelet in the same metal she'd bought at an antique fair.

But, for a girl who'd just had her heart broken, she looked good, she thought judiciously. Not a trace of blood anywhere.

And only she knew that all this was for Joel, and him alone. Her secret. Her problem. And maybe, when he looked at her, he would feel one brief instant of regret.

Or not, Darcy admitted with a silent sigh. Perhaps his sexual curiosity had been fully satisfied, and he didn't consider her worth any further effort on his part. It could be that simple. She might even have disappointed him. After all, she'd had no experience to bring to their lovemaking, and Joel was a sophisticated man. A connoisseur. Even Harry had said so.

He was running Werner Langton, and she'd been one of the perks of the job, one that he was not prepared to forgo, even if his heart belonged to another girl. Because a man did not always equate the demands of his sex drive with love, she thought sadly.

Although, if Joel had married his Emma, instinct told her that he would have been faithful and steadfast all his days. Love could do that.

He was waiting for her in the living room, leaning in the doorway and gazing out into the velvety darkness, whisky in hand. He'd pulled out all the stops too, she saw, dressed in the formality of a white tuxedo over elegant black trousers, his lean waist accentuated by a black cummerbund. He wore no tie, and his frilled dress shirt was open at the throat.

He turned when he heard the click of her heels, his brows lifting sharply as he looked at her. He said quietly, 'You take my breath away.'

For one heartbeat, she thought he was going to hold out his arms to her, but instead he asked, 'May I get you a drink?'

'No, thanks. I'll wait till we get up to the hotel.' He'd spelled out the situation to her on the beach, she thought, so it was absurd to feel so disappointed. And ludicrous to hope...

His smile was coolly friendly. 'You're probably wise to wait. Although their speciality is a lethal form of punch that Bob Ferrars calls the Barracuda. Don't let the fruit juice fool you.'

'Warning taken.' She kept her tone light. 'I'll try not to get bitten.'

He paused. 'I rang your father just now, to let him know that all's well. He sends his love, and I said you'd call him tomorrow.'

'Fine.' She was ashamed to realise that she'd barely given her father a thought since her arrival. And what would she say to him? Echo 'All's well' when she was actually falling apart?

Joel finished his whisky. 'Can you walk in those heels,' he enquired with faint amusement, 'or shall I get Vince to pick us up?'

She spun round slowly and gracefully, her skirt flaring. 'I can walk. And dance too, if I'm asked.'

'I'm sure you will be.' *But not necessarily by me.* The message reached her loud and clear. *And don't flirt with me either.*

He was probably right, she thought, wincing inwardly. Moving to music in his arms might prove an all too potent reminder of the older, secret rhythms he'd taught her last night.

And challenging him with a smile and the supple twist of her lightly clad body was unwise too. And a waste of time.

So she walked sedately beside him in the darkness, up the narrow path between the high banks of flowering shrubs, infinitely careful not to brush against him, or even touch his hand with hers.

And infinitely thankful when the bright lights of the hotel finally appeared in front of them.

Approached through the gardens at the rear, the floodlit swimming pool was directly in front of them, surrounded on three sides by the hotel building itself. All the glass doors and shutters on the ground floor were wide open, allowing tables to spill out onto the marble concourse around the pool. Chatter and laughter filled the air, underlaid by music with a soft reggae beat coming from inside the hotel.

For a moment Darcy's steps faltered. She felt self-conscious suddenly, and absurdly shy, as if all the other guests would instantly know that she was a fraud, a non-wife, and point the finger. And that was ludicrous, but it said a lot about her state of mind, she thought unhappily.

'What's wrong?' Joel asked.

'I wasn't expecting so many people,' she said ruefully. 'The bungalow's so quiet.'

'Which is why I chose it.' He took her hand, the clasp of his fingers light and impersonal. 'But you'll find the natives are friendly. A damned sight more so than the Werner Langton board,' he added drily. 'And you cope with them impeccably.' He pointed up at the wide first-floor balcony, under its thatched awning. 'We have a table up there.' He glanced at her, brows raised. 'Brave enough to face a Barracuda first?'

Darcy lifted her chin. 'Why not?'

He guided her through the busy room to the bar, which ran its entire length at the rear. Darcy perched on one of the high stools, and Joel stood, leaning against the bar, beside her. Their drinks arrived in hollowed-out pineapple shells, lavishly decorated with greenery and sliced fruit. Darcy took a cautious sip through her straw, and said, 'That's lovely,' then suddenly gasped, her eyes widening. 'My God, this thing has an aftershock off the Richter scale.'

'Barracudas don't take many prisoners.' He was grinning.

'But go slowly. Because if the worst happens, I shall not be chivalrous and carry you home. You'll lie where you fall.' He paused. 'They do great seafood here. Do you like lobster?'

She nodded. 'Love it.'

'Then that's what we'll have,' he said. 'Plain grilled, with rice Mariella, which is an invention of Bob's wife, and named for her.'

Over his shoulder, Darcy could see the manager who'd greeted them on the first evening making his way towards them.

'I am so sorry to disturb you,' he apologised. 'But Mr Castille is wanted on the telephone. It is urgent, I think.'

Joel straightened, his mouth tightening. 'I'll take it,' he said. He glanced at Darcy. 'Will you be all right?'

'Fine,' she said, rather too brightly. 'If I'm not here when you get back, just look under the stool.'

She watched him go. Saw the sideways glances he attracted, particularly from women. Guessed she would have to accustom herself to that. Although, when they went back to London, they probably wouldn't be spending a great deal of time together, not in public anyway. If entertaining was required, it would probably be done at home in Chelsea.

Except that it wasn't a home. Not any longer. It was now a company house. And hers was strictly a company marriage.

She took another sip of her drink, trying not to wonder who had telephoned. It must be someone important to elicit such a prompt response from Joel. A call he might have been expecting.

She glanced at her watch, working out the time difference with the UK, and wondered if he would tell her about the call when he got back. Or if it would be strictly private like the one he'd taken that morning.

I think, she told herself, that I'll have to become temporarily deaf and blind. Also stop asking questions, even if they're directed at myself. And she sighed inwardly, stirring her drink with its straw.

'Darcy, my pearl. What on earth are you doing here?'

She'd have recognised that deep chocolate cream voice anywhere. And run for cover, given the opportunity.

She braced herself, then turned, smiling. 'Drew,' she said. 'How nice.'

'Nice doesn't touch the surface.' Drew Maidstone was wearing blazer and flannels, and his long fair hair was combed back in its usual carefully casual style. He turned to the older, red-faced man he was with. 'Ted—meet Darcy Langton. She and I go way, way back.'

'Not that far,' Darcy said coolly. 'If you remember, I spent a very short time grafting on your boat for starvation wages.' *And nearly getting arrested into the bargain.*

He grinned, unruffled. 'Well, you don't look very starved now. Quite delectable, in fact. Was that why you left me in the lurch? Because you wanted more money?' His eyes went over her. 'You should have come and asked me, sweetie-pie. Tried the personal approach.'

She said sweetly, 'I was never that hungry.' She paused. 'What brings you to Augustina?'

'I heard Bob Ferrars had a plan to build a few houses on the other side of the island. Thought I might view the location and have a chat, but unfortunately he's away.'

He glanced round. 'Are you working here now? Are you some kind of hostess?'

'No,' Joel said. 'She's my wife.'

He seemed to have come from nowhere. Now he stood behind Darcy, his hands resting lightly on her upper arms.

'Really?' Drew's light eyes flickered over him, then sharpened. 'Why, it's Joel Castille, isn't it? We met a few years ago in Paris, when I was doing that land deal.'

'Yes,' Joel agreed. 'We did.'

'And now you've married Gavin Langton's wee chick. Well, major congratulations, old boy. She's an amazing girl.' His smile widened maliciously. 'Always used to remind me of one of those cats that hang round farm buildings, but won't come into the house. But I expect you'll soon have her domesticated.'

'No,' Joel said. 'And I wouldn't even try.' His hands tightened on Darcy's arms. 'We should really go to our table, darling, or the champagne will be getting warm.'

'We're sitting just over there. Have a drink with us,' Drew

urged. 'Ted and I would be delighted. And Darcy and I have some catching up to do.'

'Do we?' Darcy asked calmly. 'I can't imagine why.' She included the bewildered Ted in her brief formal smile as she slid down from her stool. 'And we must be going. Do have a nice evening.'

'Well,' Joel said, as they sat down at their table at the edge of the balcony. 'What a pleasant surprise for you. It's always good to meet up with old friends.'

'If ever I do,' Darcy said shortly, 'I'll let you know. Because Drew Maidstone is not in that category.' She looked at the ice bucket beside the table, her brows lifting. 'But you really did order champagne. It wasn't a joke.' She picked up a menu, and studied it resolutely. 'So, what toast are you planning tonight? To bigger and better honesty?'

'I thought to friendship,' he said. 'Perhaps.'

'Good idea,' she said. 'One can never have too many friends.' She was struggling not to grimace with pain, glad that Joel could not see her eyes.

I don't want to be friends, she wanted to scream. I want so much more. All the things that you can't give me because they belong to someone else.

I want your love.

She was glad she already knew what she planned to order, because the words on the menu were swimming in front of her, and her heart was pounding so violently she felt as if it might burst through her ribcage.

Because it had happened, she realised with sick incredulity. She'd fallen in love with Joel Castille. Except it was more than that. She loved him. Had given him her heart and soul as well as her body. And wanted him not just as her lover, but also as her husband, the father of her children. Her man until the end of time, and beyond.

Oh, God, she thought, caught hysterically between tears and laughter. Worst-case scenario ever, or what?

Was this why he'd put her at a distance? Because he'd recognised this was a possibility, and wanted to end it before it became reality? Let her down lightly?

'Are you all right?' He was watching her, eyes narrowed. 'Because for a moment there, you seemed to be somewhere else.'

'Just absorbing my surroundings.' She couldn't believe her voice sounded so normal. She looked over the balcony. 'That's an amazing pool down there.'

'The diving school use it for a couple of hours each day. I thought I'd go out on the boat later in the week, and if you booked some lessons you could come with me. We could explore the reef together.'

As friends? she thought. Substituting kindness and consideration for passion? That would be unendurable.

He added, 'I'd make sure you didn't get into any trouble.'

Under the circumstances, that was almost funny, but Darcy couldn't smile.

'It's a kind thought,' she said, 'but I'll pass.' She paused for the downright lie. 'I'm afraid I'm not a very strong swimmer.'

And I'm out of my depth already, anyway, she thought. Drowning. So I don't need the pull of an ocean to drag me down.

There was a silence, then he said, 'You surprise me,' and beckoned to their waiter to open the champagne.

Under different circumstances, it would have been a meal from paradise. The lobster, perfectly grilled, was ambrosial, and the lightly spiced rice dish, with its mix of exotic vegetables, was the ideal accompaniment.

It was by no means a silent dinner. But, Darcy realised, they were talking like polite strangers on a first date, rather than a man and woman on honeymoon, whose bodies had reached a peak of mutual ecstasy only twenty-four hours before.

Joel told her with caustic humour about some of the early setbacks he'd experienced in his career, and she described a few of the nightmare families for whom she'd been an au pair. She'd have liked to follow up with a selection of the truly ghastly guests she'd encountered on Drew's boat, but instinct warned her that this would not be a popular topic.

But at least they could make each other laugh, she thought wistfully. That had to be something.

The music she'd heard earlier was from a four-man combo,

positioned on a small raised stage in one corner of the restaurant's indoor section. They played soft jazz and blues, as well as the Caribbean sounds, and the space reserved for dancing was full most of the time.

None of the couples seemed to choose to dance even a few inches apart, Darcy noticed, emphasising that Augustina was indeed a place for lovers.

Underlining too why Joel would not invite her onto the floor. Because she no longer had any place in his arms.

Armouring herself against the pain of that knowledge, she glanced around her constantly, deliberately interested, determinedly bright, drawing his attention to people and situations she thought might amuse him. Trying, she thought, to establish a connection, however ephemeral.

But after a while, her face was beginning to ache with the strain of being cheerful.

I need, she thought, to be alone for a while.

'The shops you mentioned,' she said, as they drank their coffee. 'Are they open now?'

'Of course.' His expression was faintly sardonic. 'This is their busiest time.' He paused. 'Planning to add to your wardrobe?'

'No,' she said. 'Just looking for something to read.'

As Joel's brows lifted quizzically, she added, 'Genuinely, this time.'

'I never doubted that,' he said. 'There's no escape route from here.'

He took some notes from his wallet, and passed them to her. 'Will that be enough?'

'Far too much.' She handed most of them back. 'I'm not that fast a reader.'

The shopping mall was situated on the lower ground floor, and reached by a flight of shallow marble steps. Darcy ignored the glamorous boutiques with their displays of designer wear for all hours of the day, and night, and the bravura glitz of the jewellery stores, and went straight to the bookshop. It wasn't large, but it carried a good selection of fiction and non-fiction, and an array of international newspapers and magazines.

Darcy picked two novels that were on the best-seller list, and added a couple of biographies that had been well-reviewed in England.

On her way back to the restaurant, a blaze of shimmering peacock-blue in a boutique window caught her eyes, and, in spite of her resolve, she lingered for a moment.

It was a silk caftan, its neckline wide and deeply slashed, fastening down the front with a series of gold satin buttons loosely fastened by loops of the same colour.

On either side of the fastening was a mass of rioting flowers and leaves in exquisite gold embroidery reaching to the hem of the skirt, which was split on one side to mid-thigh.

It was an exotic and sexy piece of nonsense, and Darcy found herself wondering what Joel would make of it if she wore it the next time they spent an evening alone.

'Thinking of buying it?' Drew Maidstone asked.

Darcy spun round with a start, to find him standing behind her. 'Absolutely not,' she returned. 'I've just seen the price tag.'

'I think you should,' he said softly. 'It would be perfect for you. Why not ask that jealous husband of yours to get it? Make him pay for his pleasures.'

Darcy looked at him icily. 'Joel is not remotely jealous. He has no reason to be.'

'Over-protective, then.' He looked her over. 'I might come across later—ask you to dance, for old times' sake. See how he reacts.'

'Please don't bother,' Darcy said quietly. 'Because the answer will always be no.'

He sighed. 'Still the little icicle, my pet. But I bet Castille makes sure you melt for him. Funny,' he added meditatively. 'I'd never have had him down as the marrying kind, or that you'd be his type. Life is full of surprises,' He blew her a kiss and sauntered off.

Darcy stared after him, her bottom lip caught in her teeth. She didn't trust Drew as far as she could throw him, and knew there was every chance that he would turn up at their table, making mischievous insinuations about her past connection with him.

Only I won't be there, she resolved.

When she got back, their table was unoccupied. She looked

round and saw Joel a short distance away, leaning on the balustrade as he looked down at the swimming pool and the crowd around it, his face preoccupied.

'You took your time.' He straightened unsmilingly as Darcy joined him.

She held up her carrier bag. 'I was spoiled for choice.'

'I'm glad you're pleased,' he said courteously. He paused. 'I was going to have a brandy. Will you join me?'

'Thanks, but no,' Darcy said with equal politeness. 'Actually, I can't wait to get started on my reading. Would you mind if I called it a night, and went back to the bungalow?'

'Not at all,' he said. 'But I'm coming with you.'

'There's no need,' Darcy protested defensively. 'Stay—enjoy the rest of your evening.'

'You're not walking through the grounds alone at night.' His tone brooked no opposition. 'If you don't want my company, then Vince will take you on the buggy. Agreed?'

She bit her lip. 'As if I have a choice.'

To make sure his wishes were carried out, Joel even came down to the foyer to see her off.

'Goodnight.' For a fleeting moment, she thought he was going to kiss her, but he stepped back. 'Sleep well.'

Once she was back at the bungalow, she didn't linger, simply pouring herself a glass of chilled mineral water before going to her room.

But she knew at the same time that she would not rest. Not yet. Not until it had been established beyond all doubt that Joel would not be joining her in bed. A forlorn hope, but one she was unable to dismiss.

She tried to read, but the words seemed to dance meaninglessly in front of her.

Eventually she dozed off, only to wake with a start when she heard the front door open and close. She sat up, listening intently, waiting for his footsteps in the passage outside.

Because he might just come to her door—open it to check that she had taken his advice and was sleeping. And maybe, if she looked at him, smiled and said his name, he might stay with her.

Acting on impulse, she slipped out of bed and went over to the dressing table, discarding her nightgown on the way.

She sat down and picked up a comb, drawing it through her hair with long, rhythmic strokes. She found herself wishing that she was a mermaid on a rock, or a lorelei. That she knew some siren song that would call him to her, and keep him. And found herself whispering his name over and over again.

When she heard him walking along the passage, her breathing almost stopped, and she felt her skin warm with excitement. Anticipation.

Please let him stop, she prayed silently. Let him open my door and see me. Let him come to me.

But he didn't even pause, and the next minute she heard his own door closing. A sound of total finality.

She stared at herself in the mirror, her face crumpling like that of a bewildered child. And she knew she had never before felt so much alone.

Next morning, she had to force herself to shower and dress. She didn't want to face him. She wanted to stay in her room, and have food pushed under her door.

She couldn't think of the previous night's performance without cringing. Calling his name under her breath, for heaven's sake. How ludicrous was that? Sitting around naked on the off-chance he might call in, just as if their talk on the beach had never happened. Pathetic!

And what would she have done if he'd taken one look, and said 'Thanks, but no thanks'? And, for a moment, she felt physically sick.

She found Joel outside on the veranda, dressed in shorts and a T-shirt, drinking coffee and studying a map of the island.

'Good morning.' He rose politely to his feet. 'Did you sleep well?'

'Yes, thank you.' It was a lie. She'd hardly closed her eyes all night.

'A note came for you.' He handed her an envelope with the hotel logo on the table and resumed his seat.

She opened it, and unfolded the single sheet of paper. 'Missed you last night,' ran the message. 'Come and have lunch on the boat.' It was signed, 'Drew.'

Darcy could have screamed. Her instinct that he was out to make mischief was justified. 'Jealous,' he'd said last night. 'Over-protective.' Drew was wrong on both counts, but he didn't know that, only that they were newly married, and his attentions wouldn't be welcome.

She'd seen him in action when she worked for him, she recalled furiously, deliberately setting people at odds with each other to see what would happen. Enjoying the explosion when it came.

She wanted to tear up his damned note and jump on it, but that would give it undue importance, so she slipped it into the pocket of her overshirt instead, intending to deal with it later. She glanced at Joel as she did so, but he seemed engrossed in his map.

She said, 'Shall I make some more coffee?'

'Not for me, thanks. I'm off in a minute. I've booked some time on the dive boat this morning.' He folded the map, and put it aside. 'Would you like to come along, just for the ride? See what's involved?'

'I hardly think so,' she said quietly. 'I'd only be in the way.'

'And you probably have other plans.' His tone was silky, but Darcy wasn't deceived. He knew the note was an invitation from Drew. What he hadn't worked out was that she'd rather be boiled in oil than accept.

But you don't want me, she thought, so why should you care anyway?

'Lots of them,' she said lightly. 'I don't expect one dull moment.' *Coming to terms with a life without you will be high on the agenda.*

'Well, try and make time to call your father during this ceaseless round of enjoyment.' There was a harsh note in his voice.

'Of course,' she said. 'I'll phone Aunt Freddie too, if that's all right. Leave a message.'

'Fine.' He got to his feet, picking up the bag beside the table. 'I'll see you later.'

Diving could be dangerous. She knew that. She wanted to say, Take care. Please keep safe.

But instead, she offered him another bright, meaningless smile. 'Have fun,' she said and went indoors to make her coffee without waiting for his reply.

When she was alone, she tore the note into tiny fragments and put them in the bin. Dealt with, she thought. And now for the rest of her life.

'Darling.' Her father's voice was warm. 'Are you happy? Is Joel treating you well?'

'Everything's wonderful,' she assured him steadily. 'And this is the most beautiful place.'

'Good—good.' They chatted for a while, but it occurred to Darcy that her father seemed slightly distracted. There was a pause, then he said almost abruptly, 'I wanted to warn you, my dear, that I'll be away for a few days from tomorrow, and can't be contacted.'

'Right.' Darcy was faintly surprised at this. Her father had always been punctilious in the past about leaving addresses and telephone numbers during his absences. 'Business or pleasure?'

'Just routine. I'll be in touch as soon as I get back.'

'Fine.' She hesitated. 'I suppose it will soon be time to talk about Christmas plans.'

'There's no immediate hurry for that.' There was another silence.

Then: 'Bless you, darling. Take care always.' And he was gone.

He sounded odd, Darcy thought as she switched off the phone. Or am I just being paranoid, because the rest of my life is in such chaos?

It seemed a very long morning, and, although she swam several lengths of the pool, and read under the shade of a parasol, Darcy was unable to completely relax. Joel was in her mind all the time, and she wished now she'd swallowed her pride and gone with him on the boat.

She was getting a cold beer from the fridge, when there was a knock at the main door, and she found Vince waiting.

She said sharply, her heart thudding with dread, imagining empty tanks, sharks, giant squid, 'What's happened? Is something wrong?'

'A delivery for you, ma'am.' He produced a flat box tied with ribbons from behind his back, and handed it to her.

She began, 'There must be some mistake…' but he was already on board the buggy, and leaving with a genial wave.

Darcy undid the ribbon bow and lifted the lid, parting the folds of tissue. In the sunlight, the iridescent blue silk of the caftan glowed even more brightly.

Limply she put the box on the table, and sank down on a chair. There was no card, but she knew who'd sent it. After all, he'd caught her admiring it last night. Drew had known she wouldn't accept his lunch invitation, so he'd caught her with a double whammy, well aware of the implications of such an intimate and expensive gift.

And it was only luck that Joel wasn't here to witness its arrival, and draw his own conclusions as Drew had clearly intended.

Well, he was going to be disappointed, she told herself grimly. She found kitchen scissors and cut up the box and its ribbon, then rolled up the caftan inside its tissue wrapping and buried the lot deep in the bin. She could have wept as she did so. It was such a lovely thing, the silk feeling cool and sensuous against her fingers.

It might have made her look desirable, she thought desolately. Even irresistible. And now she would never know.

Because this was one nasty little game that Drew had to lose, although it meant there would be no victory for her either.

And that, she thought, is what I must learn to endure.

CHAPTER TWELVE

SHE HAD herself well under control when Joel returned, greeting him with a cool smile as he came out to the poolside, beer in hand. 'Hi—was the reef as good as you hoped?'

'Better.' He stripped down to his swimming trunks, and stretched out on an adjoining lounger. 'Sure I can't persuade you to have some lessons?'

If you loved me, and wanted our marriage to work, she thought, you could persuade me to jump out of an aircraft without a parachute.

'Separate paths,' she said. 'Remember? In fact, I called Reception and booked myself some tennis coaching instead,' she added airily. 'So we're both catered for.' She paused. 'And they told me when the boat was due back, so I ordered some grilled fish for lunch. It should be here any time now.'

'How incredibly efficient,' Joel drawled, a slight edge to his tone.

'Well,' she said, 'I have to justify my existence somehow.' She paused again. 'I thought you'd be pleased.'

He said flatly, 'I'm delighted.' He swung himself off the lounger, walked to the side of the pool, and dived in.

Well, you could have fooled me! She wanted childishly to shout it after him, but didn't.

So, what was his problem? she demanded silently. She was trying damned hard to behave well. She hadn't thrown herself at him, or made terrible scenes, or even let him find her weeping quietly in a corner. She was attempting to cut herself off from any kind of dependence on him, and behave civilly at the same time.

It wasn't easy, and she didn't expect lavish praise, but he might have been marginally grateful.

She was almost sorry that the caftan had been removed with the rest of the rubbish an hour before.

I should have flaunted it, she thought. Let him see that someone wants me, even though he doesn't. Except it's not true, she amended ruefully. Drew is just one of nature's troublemakers, and Joel would simply end up thinking badly of me all over again.

But there was clearly something wrong. Maybe Joel was just realising what a really awful idea this honeymoon was, forcing him into close proximity with a girl he didn't love, and now no longer wanted.

It doesn't get much worse than that, she thought, watching him cover length after length with his strong, expert crawl. And all I can do is keep out of his way as much as possible. Play tennis. Go riding. Even learn to paint, and astonish Aunt Freddie when I go home.

Also, go to the hotel's medical centre and ask the doctor for something to knock me out at night. So that I can forget Joel is sleeping only a few yards away from me.

There are ways of dealing with the situation, she thought, and I'll find one that might even work for us both.

The tennis session was almost brutal, requiring all her concentration, but Darcy was glad of it. She booked another lesson for the following day, stating mendaciously that she wanted to improve her game to surprise her husband. She told the doctor at the medical centre that the heat was keeping her awake, and received an astonished look along with a strictly limited supply of sleeping pills.

'I don't get asked for these too often,' he said. 'Not here. Is anything else troubling you apart from the heat?'

'Nothing.' *Apart from a broken heart, and no amount of chemical intervention can deal with that.*

'Hm.' His look was kind but searching. 'Then maybe you should just try and relax a little more. Go with the flow.'

When she returned to the bungalow, she found Joel working

on his laptop. To her surprise, he announced abruptly that they'd be dining at the bungalow that evening.

'Oh.' She hesitated. 'I thought we'd be going back to the restaurant.' *A public place with other people around.*

He said flatly, 'You'd rather do that?'

It would be so much easier to bear than being alone with you.

'It has a marvellous atmosphere,' she said, shrugging. 'Also I like the band.'

'Tomorrow, perhaps,' he said. 'I thought after your exertions on the tennis courts, you might prefer a quiet dinner tonight.'

Darcy set off towards her bedroom. 'Whatever you say,' she tossed back over her shoulder. 'It really doesn't matter.'

But it does, she thought achingly. It matters terribly, but only to me.

She'd just emerged from the bathroom, when he tapped on her door to tell her he'd poured her a drink. She put on the towelling dressing gown, belted it tightly, and went reluctantly to join him.

He was wearing his robe too, his hair still damp from the shower, and she felt the painful rake of memory at the sight of him. And the harsh, deep clench of desire. When he turned to hand her the glass of wine he paused suddenly, his dark brows lifting. 'Still wearing the shroud, I see.' The comment was abrupt. 'I thought you'd have replaced it by now.'

'I don't think I shall bother,' she said, her cheeks warming faintly as she thought of the caftan. 'This serves its purpose perfectly well.' She took her wine with a word of thanks, and sipped.

'Yes,' he said slowly. 'I'm beginning to see that it does.' He looked down at himself, his mouth twisting in a self-mockery that was almost bitter.

'I thought, as we were dining here…' He stopped, then added, 'I feel seriously underdressed. I'll go and put something else on.'

Darcy watched him go with faint puzzlement. He seemed almost annoyed about something. She could only hope that he hadn't been embarrassed because he'd caught her looking at him with too obvious a longing.

She would need, she thought, to be more circumspect in future.

He came back presently, lean and attractive in close-fitting olive trousers and a black polo shirt, open at the throat, and Darcy wondered if there would ever be a time when her heartbeat wouldn't quicken at the sight of him.

The arrival of the food provided her with a much-needed diversion. There was a fish terrine to start with, followed by Chicken Augustina, a hot and spicy casserole dish, accompanied by sweet-potato fritters. The dessert was a creamy coconut tart.

'I hope you're hungry,' Joel said as they sat down.

Starved, she thought, famished. But not for food...

It was not the easiest of meals. Conversation between them was sporadic at best, with Joel still seemingly lost in his own thoughts.

However, she managed to eat with an approximation of her usual healthy appetite, and was able to praise the food with total sincerity when dinner was over.

'I thought tomorrow we could rent a Jeep,' he said, as they drank their coffee. 'Go round the island, find a quiet beach and picnic. We could even treasure-hunt. Legend says that Blackbeard stashed some of his loot here.'

'Perhaps another day. I already have plans for tomorrow.' She kept her tone cool to the point of indifference, and saw his mouth tighten.

He said, 'If they involve Drew Maidstone, you'll be disappointed. I gather he left for Antigua this afternoon.'

'What a shame,' she said. 'I'd have liked another chat.' *I'd also like to have stamped on his feet and spat in his eye, and I've lost that opportunity too.*

She lifted her chin, looked back at him. 'But please don't concern yourself about me. I'm not a child who has to be entertained.'

'I'm sorry if I gave that impression,' he returned quietly. 'I was hoping we might be able to move forward a little, maybe even become friends.'

'Most friendships are forged over many years,' she said. 'I doubt we'll have time for that.'

She got to her feet. 'However, you were right about the tennis. I'm completely knocked out, so an early night beckons.'

'Of course.' He rose too. The blue eyes were remote as they

went over her. 'You don't mind if I go up to the hotel for a drink, I hope? I'll try not to make too much noise when I come back. I wouldn't wish to disturb you.'

She shrugged. 'You're very considerate, but please don't worry. When I'm asleep, the band of the Coldstream Guards marching past couldn't wake me.' *And tonight I will sleep.* I've made quite sure of that.

I must be, she thought, the only bride who needs to take sleeping tablets on honeymoon.

She forced a smile. 'Goodnight,' she said, and turned away.

Darcy woke late the following morning, her head muzzy, her mind reeling from the memory of wild and disturbing dreams. She drenched herself under a cool shower, then dressed in shorts and a sleeveless top, braiding her still damp hair into a plait.

The living room was empty, and she presumed that Joel had already left for another morning's exploration of the glories of the reef.

She poured herself some orange juice, and gulped it down. She needed to organise a complete avoidance strategy, she told herself. Book a whole course with the tennis coach instead of individual lessons. Enquire about the island treks on horseback. Fill her days.

The evenings, of course, would always be trickier, but the hotel had more than one place to eat, and she'd suggest to Joel that they try them in turn. Eat alone, if she had to. But there'd be no more tête-à-tête suppers at the bungalow, especially if, as last night, he didn't always plan to dress for dinner.

She walked up to the hotel, taking her time, breathing in the fragrance of the flowers and shrubs around her, listening to the ever-present whisper of the sea. It could, she thought, have been paradise, if only…

And stopped right there, wincing at the thoughts she could not permit herself, and the longings she had to subdue.

She was heading across the foyer to Reception, when she realised with shock that Joel was there before her. Not on the dive boat at all, but standing in the glass booth at the far end of the long desk, his back half-turned, head bent, talking on the public phone.

She halted instantly, staring at him, her mind whirling. So what calls were so private, or so urgent that he needed to make them from here instead of the bungalow—unless he wished to ensure that she could not possibly overhear what was being said?

If he looked round, he would see her at once. Maybe think she'd followed him, and was spying on him. And she couldn't bear that.

In fact, she couldn't bear any of it, she thought as she did a swift U-turn and dived down the stairs to the shopping mall. She didn't want to shop, but it was a place to hide until Joel finished his secret conversation, and went.

They'd re-dressed the window in the boutique near the bookshop, but, although the new display was lovely, there was nothing to match the previous centre-piece.

Acting on impulse, she went in. 'I saw a blue caftan here,' she told the smiling woman who advanced to meet her. 'I was wondering if you had any others like it.'

'I wish I did.' The other woman shrugged regretfully. 'But they're all totally individual—designed and hand-sewn strictly one at a time. And the lady who makes them won't be hurried. I may not get another for a month or more. And when I do, I'll have it in my window for just a couple of hours before it goes. Why, I could have sold the blue one a dozen times over.'

'It was incredibly beautiful,' Darcy said, riven with guilt. All that creative dedication—all that work, she thought, and she'd thrown it away. Oh, *damn* Drew Maidstone.

'But so was the lady it was bought for, at least according to the gentleman who paid the bill.' The woman's dark eyes twinkled wickedly. She lowered her voice confidentially. 'He was really something, so I hope they both got the pleasure from it that he had in mind.'

'The answer to that is—no,' Darcy returned with cool clarity. 'And, believe me, he is not even marginally as charming as he can seem.'

And she walked away, leaving the saleswoman staring after her, open-mouthed.

When she reached the foyer again, Joel was nowhere to be seen. Biting her lip, Darcy went over to the desk.

'I'd like to book a block of tennis lessons,' she told the recep-
tionist. 'An hour a day for the remainder of my time here, in the
name of Castille.'

'Mrs Castille?' The man looked at her oddly, but he reached
across for the coaching timetable and studied it. 'Shall we say
for tomorrow and the next day, as your plans are so fluid?'

Darcy stared at him. 'I'm afraid I don't follow.'

He looked faintly embarrassed. 'I'm sorry, Mrs Castille, but
according to your husband, you may be checking out quite soon
and returning to England.' He paused awkwardly. 'I assumed you
knew that.'

'I only know I married a workaholic.' Somehow she managed
to sound calm, even amused. 'I expect he's wondering right now
how to tell me that he's needed back at the office. As for the tennis, I'll stick with today's arrangement and then wait and see.'

There was open relief in his answering smile. 'I hope we'll
see you both again at another time, Mrs Castille.'

He probably thought that might happen, Darcy thought as she
walked away. After all, this was a place where people came to
be happy. He had no idea that Joel had simply chosen to cut his
losses and call time on their make-believe marriage.

Or that she would be going home to unbearable heartache and
loneliness.

She could only guess that this morning's mysterious phone
call had prompted Joel's decision. She remembered the brief
snatch of conversation she'd overheard on their first morning,
when he'd clearly been speaking to a woman. He'd called her
'darling', and Darcy had known at once that it must be Emma.

Emma, that precious part of his life. The girl he loved, but
couldn't have because she was someone else's wife, for good or ill,
and about to have his baby. Something Joel had to learn to live with.

She wondered if he'd called her 'darling' again. Told her he
missed her and that he'd be back soon.

She would never know, because she could never ask. Only accept. Then go on pretending, somehow, that it didn't matter.
That she even welcomed her new-found freedom.

She wrapped her arms round her body, but it was no defence
against the pain that tore at her.

She'd hated Joel once. Perhaps she could learn to do so again. Force herself to forget how he had become as necessary to her as breath itself.

And that, without him, she was going to be lost in a wilderness of endless desolation.

Suddenly she knew she couldn't go back to the bungalow, because Joel might be there, and she couldn't face him, not yet. Couldn't bear to hear what he had to say.

Instead, she headed for the bar, climbing onto one of the high stools at the counter. The barman stopped polishing glasses, and came over.

'What can I get you, ma'am? A beer, a coffee?'

'No,' she said. 'I'd like a Barracuda.'

It was clearly her day for surprising people, because his jaw almost dropped, and she saw him take a surreptitious glance at his watch, but he concocted the mixture and brought it to her.

She took a deep breath, gulped some of the drink through her straw and felt it hit. She waited for a count of ten, then drank again.

'Isn't it a little early in the day for that?' Joel sounded faintly amused as he took the stool beside her.

Darcy hadn't been aware of his approach. Couldn't fathom how he'd tracked her down either. Her heart was thudding violently, but she managed to speak with relative calm. 'That might depend on the kind of day you're going to have.'

'Well,' he said, 'there is an alternative to sitting here, getting blasted.'

He signalled to the barman to bring him a beer. When he spoke again, his voice was quiet. 'Darcy, I realise bringing you here wasn't the best idea I've ever had. The atmosphere's a little too intense for our situation. I know you didn't seem keen last night, but I still think we should get away for a few hours.'

He paused. 'The crowd I went diving with are organising a trip to the other side of the island, nothing fancy, just a barbecue on the beach, swimming and some music. They've invited us along, and it could be a good idea. You'd see something of Augustina, and you wouldn't have to be alone with me.'

'Thank you,' she said. 'But I already have a date. With another Barracuda. However, there's nothing to stop you going.'

'They asked both of us,' he said, his tone almost rueful. 'If I turn up alone again, they'll begin to wonder if I really have a wife.'

She drank again. 'But you don't. You have an arrangement. Another of your really bad ideas.' She sent him a swift brittle smile. 'But one we can put right very soon. So have a nice day.'

For a long moment he stared at her as if he'd never seen her before, then he threw a handful of money on the bar beside his untouched beer and went.

Darcy stayed where she was for a while, mindlessly stirring her drink with its straw, aware that she was physically unable to swallow another mouthful. And that she wanted, very badly, to weep.

At last, moving almost numbly, she got down from her stool, and went slowly back to the bungalow.

She didn't allow herself to cry, even though she felt more alone that day than she'd ever been in her life before.

Joel, it seemed, had taken her at her word, and gone on the trip. Yet she couldn't have gone with him, she told herself defensively, and played the part of a happy bride in front of a crowd of strangers.

Because she'd run out of pretence, and no fresh supplies were expected.

It was evening when he eventually returned. Darcy had showered and changed into a plain black shift dress, and she looked up from the book she was pretending to read as he came into the living room, her heart contracting painfully.

Her lips felt stiff. 'Was—was it a good party?'

'You should have come with me,' he said. 'Then you'd have found out.' He added icily, 'I booked a table in the restaurant, on the assumption you're still prepared to eat in my company. But it can always be cancelled.'

'No,' she said. 'No, that's fine.'

He nodded and went to his room, emerging a short while afterwards in close-fitting cream trousers, and a blue shirt.

They walked up to the hotel in silence.

'Are you still on Barracudas?' he asked as they went into the bar.

Darcy suppressed a shudder. 'White wine, please. Dry.'

Up in the restaurant, Joel ordered steak, and she said she'd have the same, because it was easier than feigning an interest in what was on offer. And when it came she would make herself eat it too, she resolved silently. However, the tender succulence of the meat made that less of a problem than she'd expected.

As she ate she became aware she was being watched from an adjoining table by a petite but glamorous redhead, showing off a superb tan in a white dress hardly larger than a table napkin, and that others in the crowd at the same table were also turning round to look at them.

'People you know?' she asked Joel, as he returned a wave.

'The gang I was with today. Come on over, and I'll introduce you.' He rose, extending a hand, but Darcy remained where she was.

'I'll pass, if you don't mind. I was about to go back to the bungalow.'

'Again?' He stared down at her. 'I was hoping you'd stay. That we might dance.'

The thought jolted her heart. She gave a slight shake of the head, touching her fingertips to her temples. 'I think I spent too much time in the sun today.' She gave a brief, taut smile. 'But don't let me stop you.'

'Don't worry,' Joel returned harshly. 'You won't.'

She watched him walk over to the table to a barrage of noisy greetings, and sit down next to the redhead, whose sulky mouth was now wearing a ravishing smile.

Darcy refilled her glass with mineral water, and drank every drop. When she looked again, she saw that Joel was now on the dance floor, his partner's sinuous little body pressed against him and her arms twined round his neck.

Time I wasn't here, she told herself, reaching for her bag.

The path down to the bungalow was familiar now, and Darcy walked it almost on autopilot.

She seemed to be learning the hard way to be a realist. To accept that hers wasn't a real marriage, so that Joel wasn't bound by the usual rules. And that even his love for Emma wouldn't prevent him from finding sexual consolation when he needed it.

Celibacy would have no appeal for him. Because he was a realist too, and would take his pleasure where he found it. And not always with the woman he'd married for convenience.

Knowing that was one thing. Actually seeing him with another woman in his arms was very different.

Her head was beginning to ache in earnest, so she swapped her sleeping pills for some painkillers, and went to bed. Against all odds, she went to sleep almost at once, only to wake with a start several hours later.

She lay, watching the moonlight across the floor, and wondering what had disturbed her. Joel returning, perhaps.

Or maybe she was just uncomfortable, and thirsty. She pushed away the sheet and got up, her nightgown clinging to her sweat-dampened body, and went quietly in search of some water.

On her way back, acting on an impulse she barely understood, she opened Joel's door and looked in. But the room and the bed were both empty.

Her husband, apparently, was spending the night elsewhere.

I asked for it, she thought. I turned him loose, but that makes it no easier to bear.

Feeling suddenly stifled, she returned to her own room and pushed open the door shutters. She stepped outside, barefoot, hoping vainly for a faint breeze, but it was just as hot and still as it was indoors.

She found her gaze travelling with sudden yearning to the shimmer of the pool a few yards away.

Well, she thought. Why not?

She slipped down the straps of her nightgown, and let the garment drop to the ground. Then she walked over, and slid with a little sigh into the water. She'd never swum naked before, so its caress against her overheated skin was a new delight.

She swam one smooth length, then turned on her back, and let herself drift.

She was never sure when she realised she was no longer alone. When she saw Joel standing motionless at the side of the pool, his face absorbed, stark in the moonlight as he watched her.

Immediately she submerged, trying to hide herself but knowing that it was far too late. And that when she resurfaced, gasping and pushing back her drenched hair, he would still be there. Waiting.

Slowly she swam to the edge, and he reached down, fitting his hands under her armpits, lifting her free of the water as easily as if she'd been a child. Placing her in front of him, only a few inches away.

She found herself looking up into his eyes, the breath catching in her throat at what she saw there. And totally unable to look away. To speak. Or to save herself.

Instead, her hands slid to his shoulders and upwards, locking round his neck as she drew him down to her. And she heard her own soft moan of abandonment as his mouth took hers with a passionate hunger that bordered on savagery, and beyond.

Darcy's lips felt burning, almost swollen when Joel raised his head at last. For a moment, they stared at each other as if dazed. Then, silently, he took her hand and led her over to the sun loungers, removing the thick, cushioned mattresses and throwing them to the ground.

As he straightened she reached for him, struggling frantically to deal with the fastenings on his clothing.

'Wait.' His voice was hoarse, shaken. He stripped himself swiftly, shrugging away his shirt, dragging off his trousers and briefs. Uncovering himself so that she could touch him, press her lips to his naked flesh. 'There—ah, my love, my love, there!'

His own hands were touching her everywhere, caressing her cool, damp skin, cupping her breasts, sliding over her flanks and the smooth swell of her buttocks. Then parting her thighs to reach the molten core of her, his fingers stroking and inflaming until she cried out, her voice thick with desire. Until his mouth silenced her, moving on hers with warm, deliberate sensuality.

Still kissing her, he sank down onto the cushions, drawing her down after him, astride him. His hands clasped her hips as he lowered her with heart-stopping slowness, until all the hot, aroused strength of him was accepted, welcomed within her.

And Darcy gasped as she felt her body close round him, hold him. As she experienced for the first time this devastating intensity of sensation.

'Are you all right?' His whisper was husky. He lifted a hand, pushing the damp tangle of hair back from her face.

'Yes.' Her own voice was a thread. 'But I'm afraid of hurting you.'

His eyes were sublimely tender. 'You won't.'

His fingers caressed her shoulders, then slid down her spine, so that she arched towards him, catching her breath, her sensitised skin shivering deliciously.

She bent to him, kissing his eyelids, his cheekbones and his mouth, letting the tip of her tongue penetrate his lips, teasing sensuously, as she tested the power of her own sexuality and felt the swift surge of his response.

Then, shyly at first, she began to move, her initial inhibitions slipping away as she heard Joel groan softly with satisfaction. As some new-found female instinct offered her a rhythm, deep and insistent, and showed her how to exploit it in the slow, voluptuous rise and fall of her body—the languorous grind of her hips.

As she discovered with wonder that she could control the muscles inside her body, and use them to clench round his rigid shaft, then give him sensuous release.

His hands were on her breasts, stroking them, holding their delicate roundness in his palms as he played with her hardening nipples, watching her through half-closed eyes, his head thrown back and the line of his throat taut.

There was a wildness building in her blood, an exultancy at the rapturous physicality of their union, and this heated, sensual delight they were creating for each other.

She was free, flying, her senses going crazy. And the ultimate sweetness was close, so close, yet just out of reach.

She could hear the tortured rasp of Joel's breathing mingled with the harsh sob of her own, and then his hand slid over her thigh, gliding inward to the joining of their bodies, to seek her tiny, moist pinnacle and caress it gently with a fingertip.

Splintering the last remnants of control, and sending her over the edge into some undreamed-of glory.

Darcy could hear herself crying out deliriously, her voice rising almost to a scream as the pounding spasms of delight convulsed her. Her whole body was bucking wildly, prolonging this fierce ecstasy to its limit in the knowledge that she was taking him with her. And feeling, deep inside her, the scalding heat of him as he came.

When awareness finally returned, she was lying slumped across his body, her face buried in the curve of his neck, her sweat mingling with his. But as she stirred, and began to sit up, self-consciousness came creeping back to plague her, and, as though he sensed this, Joel's fingers captured her chin and gently drew her mouth to his.

The kiss was slow and sweet, like a benediction, and her lips trembled against his.

When they eventually drew apart, Darcy turned away a little, sitting with her head bowed on her bent knee as she waited for her breathing to return to normal. Joel reached a lazy arm for his discarded shirt, and wrapped it round her.

He said softly, 'How can you give so much joy and still not want to look at me? Or for me to look at you? Don't you know how beautiful you are?'

Mutely, she shook her head, feeling her face burn.

There was a smile in his voice. 'Then I shall have to keep proving it to you, until you believe me.'

He got to his feet, pulling her up with him.

'What are you doing?' She tried to hang back, but his arm was firm around her, urging her towards his bedroom.

'What I should have done every day and night since we arrived,' he said. 'Taking you to bed.'

CHAPTER THIRTEEN

IT WAS a time borrowed from paradise. A time for learning that sexual exhaustion did not last, but was only a prelude to even more pleasure, feeding off itself to create new appetites, new desires. A time to discover that her own powers of recovery were almost shamingly swift, and her capacity for passion frank and hungry.

And Joel taught her these things with a skill and artistry that, more than once, overwhelmed her, and left her sobbing with delight in his arms.

And as she finally drifted off to sleep, her head pillowed on his chest, she found herself wondering how she could ever have imagined she would not want him, close to her in the night like this.

But, she discovered with disappointment as she opened drowsy eyes on another glorious, sunlit day, he was not still beside her when she woke.

And she'd wanted him to be there, she realised. Wanted to lie wrapped in his arms while they talked, said all the things there'd been no time for last night. Made plans...

She stirred suddenly, restlessly. She was allowing herself to think that everything had changed, that this was a whole new beginning for them both. But there was no actual evidence of that.

She and Joel had made love. More accurately, perhaps, they'd had sex, and for her it had been an incredible, unforgettable experience. Whereas for him, she might have been just another eager female body.

Like the redhead, she thought. She'd assumed Joel was with her last night, but she'd been wrong. There'd been no other woman's scent on his clothing and skin, so he'd decided to draw back, or perhaps the redhead had.

And when he came back he found me swimming naked in the pool, she thought, and what followed I myself started when I kissed him. When I made it so obvious I was crazy for him. I was—available, and Joel took what was on offer, and made it wonderful. And I don't doubt he'll continue to do so while we stay married, if I let him see that I'm willing.

But it hasn't changed anything. Joel married me to get Werner Langton, and because he can't have the woman he loves. Emma is still there, between us, and she always will be.

I'll only ever be a temporary substitute, and I know that. I've told myself so over and over again. So how could I have allowed myself to forget so easily?

Because Joel certainly hasn't forgotten, and that's why he's never once said 'I love you'. And if last night had made even the slightest difference to that, he'd have been here beside me this morning.

In spite of the warmth of the day, she was shivering. She left the bed, winding the sheet around her, sarong-style, and went out onto the patio. The pool which had caused all the trouble was sparkling enticingly. The cushions had been replaced on the loungers, and the discarded clothes had vanished.

Everything back the way it had been. And she needed to behave as if nothing much had happened too, and not let Joel suspect, even for a moment, that she'd dreamed of so much more.

She showered and dressed in a white linen skirt and a jade strapless top, before going to the kitchen to make some coffee.

Joel's continued absence was beginning to disturb her. Unless he'd woken up blaming himself for letting his physical needs betray his heart, she thought with a pang, and had disappeared to once again walk off his guilt along the beach.

She was pouring the coffee into a beaker when the phone rang, startling her, making her splash a few drops onto her hand.

'Damn.' Sucking at the tiny scald, she grabbed up the receiver with her other hand.

'Joel?' It was a girl's voice, and it sounded as if she was crying. 'Joel, I really need you. You said you'd be back. I—I've served the divorce papers, and it's been awful. When will I see you?'

Darcy stood very still, the telephone to her ear, the back of her hand still pressed to her mouth. She could feel her lips trembling against her skin, as any small lingering hope that she might have been wrong flickered and died. Instead, all her worst fears were being brutally confirmed, and she could have moaned aloud with the anguish of it.

'Joel?' The name was almost sobbed.

Darcy found a voice from somewhere. Managed by some miracle to keep it steady. 'I'm sorry. He's not here right now. But I'll…'

She'd intended to say 'Pass your message on', but there was a shocked pause, an audible gasp, and then the connection was hurriedly cut.

If a woman answers, hang up, Darcy thought bitterly as she replaced her own receiver. She was trembling so much, she sank down onto the sofa and sat motionless, gazing into space.

Emma, she thought. Emma, Harry's wife, dear God, his pregnant wife, was getting a divorce. She'd be able to remarry, if she wished. And if the man she wanted was also free…

She stopped there, her mind going into free-fall.

How could Joel do it? she asked herself. How could he marry me, knowing that Emma planned to end her marriage so soon? Marry me and then be so cynical, so devoid of all decency, as to make love to me?

Did he really want to take my father's place at Werner Langton so much that he was prepared to make any sacrifice?

And, on their wedding night, he'd talked about honesty…

She put her hands over her face, and stayed like that for a long time. But, at last, she managed to organise herself into something like a course of action. She would say nothing about Emma's call. Judging by the girl's reaction when she realised she was talking to her lover's wife, she'd breached some kind of agreed protocol to make it, and wouldn't wish to admit as much to Joel.

And as soon as he came back, she would tell him she wanted

to return home as soon as it could be arranged. And before he could tell her the same thing.

A face-saving exercise, she thought bleakly, which would do nothing to dispel the humiliation aching inside her. The bewildered realisation of what a naïve fool she'd been.

And finally, she could never allow Joel Castille to come near her, or touch her again, or she would be lost, destroyed, smashed into a million tiny pieces.

But when she heard his footsteps crossing the veranda a few minutes later, her courage nearly failed her. She made herself stand up, clenching her fists at her sides.

Her first thought was that he looked terrible. He was pale under his tan, and his mouth was taut.

She said jerkily, 'Joel, there's something I have to say.'

'Then it will have to keep.' His voice was clipped, harsh. 'Because we have to fly back to Britain today, which doesn't leave a lot of time to pack and get out of here.'

'I know.' She looked at the floor. 'There was—a call.'

He swore under his breath. 'And I gave strict instructions that none were to be put through—until I'd had a chance to talk to you.'

He paused. 'Bob and Mariella came back last night, and their helicopter will take us straight to the airport. He's managed to get us seats—God knows how—on the evening flight. I suppose he told them it was an emergency.'

'Heavens,' she said. 'What lengths would he go to in a real crisis?'

He was walking towards her, but that halted him. 'A real crisis?' he repeated slowly. 'You don't think your father being in Intensive Care in the Royal Alexandra Clinic is a real crisis?'

She cried out, her face blanching. 'What are you talking about? He can't be ill. He's always had wonderful health.'

'Not,' Joel said more gently, 'for a while.' He crossed to the sofa and sat, patting the cushion beside him. 'Come here,' he said, 'and I'll tell you.'

'I can hear perfectly well from here.' She was rigid, unmoving. 'What's happened?'

'It's his heart. He's had several scares—what he described as "wake-up calls" during the past year,' Joel said. 'Mostly while you were working away.' His mouth tightened. 'On Drew Maidstone's boat.'

'So that was why I was summoned home,' she said tautly. 'And why I was parcelled up and handed over to you with such indecent haste.'

Something came and went in his eyes. 'If that's how you want to see it.' He added grimly, 'He decided to have his operation while we were away. Planned to call you with good news when it was over. But there were—complications.'

'I was kept in the dark,' she said, slowly. 'But you—knew all along?'

'He wanted me to take the job. I had to be told.'

'Oh, God.' She remembered with horror the flippant remark she'd once made to her aunt about pall-bearers and a memorial service. 'Why not me?'

'He wanted to protect you. Taking care of you has always been one of his main priorities. You know that.'

'Why, yes,' she said. 'Clearly, right down to arranging another caretaker for me if the worst happened. You should have warned him you had less permanent plans. Let him find someone more long-term to run his company.'

There was a silence, then Joel said quietly, 'Do you intend to stand there trying to score points, or shall we catch this plane?'

'Yes, of course.' She turned away. 'I'll go and pack.'

Joel got to his feet, his hands descending on her shoulders, pulling her towards him. She began to struggle, hands braced against him to push him away.

'No.' Her voice choked. 'No. Don't touch me, don't you dare to touch me.'

'What the hell do you think I'm going to do, jump on you?' He stared down at her with incredulity, and the beginnings of anger. 'I know you're in shock, but give me credit for some sensitivity. I just want to hold you, darling. To comfort you, if I can.' He paused, then added evenly, 'And maybe reassure myself that the warm, passionate girl in my arms last night was real, and not a figment of my imagination.'

'And I simply want to get away from here.' She didn't have to add 'And from you'. The unspoken words seemed to reverberate between them in the silence as if she'd shouted them aloud, and she saw his eyes narrow.

But he released her instantly, stepping backwards, raising his hands in an ironic gesture of surrender. He said, 'Then that's what we'll do.'

As she walked away across the living room, he said, 'That call you mentioned; who made it?'

'It's not important,' she said. 'All that matters now is my father. Just him. Nothing and no one else.' And she went into her room and closed the door.

It was cold and wet when they arrived back in Britain. It had been a difficult, edgy flight with Darcy sitting beside Joel as if she'd been strait-jacketed, desperate to avoid even the slightest touch. Knowing, at the same time, that he must be perfectly aware of her tension. Of her need to stay apart from him. Their verbal exchanges, too, had been kept to an absolute minimum, and she hoped he would rationalise this as anxiety over her father, and not demand any other explanation. Because she wasn't sure what she could say.

Joel's driver met them at the airport and drove them straight to the clinic, where a hollow-eyed Aunt Freddie was waiting. Darcy had been warned that Gavin was heavily sedated, but she was still shocked by the wires and tubes connecting his unconscious form to the electronic equipment beside the bed. For such a big man, he seemed…diminished somehow. She swayed slightly as dizziness swept her, then stiffened as Joel's hands came down on her shoulders, steadying her.

She said harshly, 'I'm all right,' and shook him off, conscious of Aunt Freddie's swift, bewildered glance in their direction.

They didn't stay long. Darcy arranged to return the following morning, when she would be able to talk to her father, and also meet with Sir Charles, the consultant in charge of the case, who was one of her father's oldest friends.

She invited her aunt to come back to Chelsea for dinner, but Freddie refused gently. 'I'll stay here for a while longer, I think. Besides,' she added, 'this is still officially your honeymoon. You don't need guests.'

As they walked down the endless corridors to the exit, Joel said, 'You should have told her.'

Her head turned sharply. 'What do you mean?'

'That the honeymoon seems to be well and truly over.' He paused, glancing at his watch. 'I'll tell Vic to drive you back, and I'll get a cab. I have a couple of things to see to.'

'Yes, of course.' Her voice sounded insanely bright as they emerged into the chill gloom of the November late afternoon. 'Then I'll see you later.'

He opened the rear passenger door of the car for her, but thankfully made no attempt to touch her, or even to help her in. As they drove off she looked back, and saw that he was standing in the same place, but not watching her go.

Instead, his cellphone was clamped to his ear, and he was totally concentrated on the conversation he'd just begun, his lips moving urgently.

And no prizes for guessing whom he was calling, and whose concerns were top of his own agenda, Darcy thought, and her teeth sank into her lower lip until she tasted blood.

At the house, she was greeted by a concerned Mrs Inman, bleating with anxiety about Gavin, and had to spend some time offering comfort and reassurance, which managed to distance her own problems, at least for a while.

She drank the tea the housekeeper tearfully provided, insisting on sharing it with her. Then, as soon as the older woman disappeared to start preparations for dinner, Darcy went upstairs. She could usefully fill the time by unpacking, she thought, but when she got to her room her case wasn't there. Moreover, she found the bed had been stripped, and the wardrobes and drawers emptied.

She swallowed. She knew, of course, where all her things would have been taken. To the master suite, so recently vacated by Gavin. The rooms it was assumed she'd now be sharing with Joel.

Except that was not going to happen, and poor Mrs Inman was just going to have to cope with yet another shock.

But she would do the donkey work herself, she decided, gritting her teeth. She didn't want to embarrass the housekeeper by involving her directly in her confrontation with Joel.

She walked into the master bedroom, freshly papered and painted in cream and gold, deliberately averting her gaze from the wide bed, with its double complement of pillows and the new quilted coverlet in glowing russet silk.

All the clothes and possessions she'd brought with her had been put away with Joel's in the adjoining dressing room.

She worked with steady purpose, transferring everything back again to her old room, then fetched sheets and pillowcases and made up the bed. The process didn't take nearly as long as she'd expected. Not a great deal of time at all, she told herself ironically, to close such a momentous chapter in her life.

Especially when she had no idea what might lie ahead of her, she admitted wearily, and found herself sighing.

She had just finished changing for dinner when Joel returned. She was aware of his voice in the hall speaking to Mrs Inman, then heard him coming upstairs and going along to his room. Their room, or so he would think.

Her hand was shaking suddenly, but she forced herself to go on brushing her hair, looking at her reflection with an assumption of calm. She'd put on a dark red dress, high-necked and long-sleeved, hoping that it would give her drained face some colour, but it seemed to have had the opposite effect. She looked, she thought critically, paler than ever.

Yet, moving to her own room again was no big deal, she told herself. Under the circumstances, he would surely expect nothing else. So there was no need to be nervous. No need at all.

Then, in the mirror, she saw him standing in the doorway behind her. She saw the bleak, dark face, the compressed mouth, the glitter in the blue gaze, and knew that she'd made a terrible— a fundamental mistake about that.

And that she should not merely be nervous, but downright scared.

All the same, she tried for a nonchalant note. 'Hi. I arranged dinner for nine. I hope that's all right.'

Joel dismissed dinner with a brief, succinct obscenity. His voice was soft, but she knew that it would have reached her from a million miles away.

Reached her and chilled her.

'Just what do you think you're playing at?'

'There's no game.' She picked up a scent spray, and put it down again. 'You said yourself that the honeymoon was over. So from now on, where you're concerned, I intend to maintain my distance, day and night.'

'To hell with the honeymoon.' His mouth hardened. 'You're my wife, Darcy, and I expect you to continue to share my bed. Starting tonight.'

'Oh, dear,' she said, lightly. 'Don't say you've wasted your money on a fresh supply of condoms.'

His head went back as if she'd struck him across the face, and she knew she'd gone too far, but the words could not be unsaid. Because it was too late. It was all much too late.

And especially too late to run to him, to throw herself into his arms and weep and weep, begging him to love her, until he picked her up and held her close and safe forever. Because it would never be like that between them.

He was legally entitled to have sex with her, and that was what he wanted. After all, she'd been willing last night. He'd see no reason why she shouldn't continue to be available, whenever he wished.

But she knew with utter certainty that she had to separate herself from him physically. Prepare herself for the time when his lips and hands would no longer touch her with desire, and he would be gone from her life.

Because she needed, somehow, to survive.

And she knew she should be glad of the coldness between them as they had left the hospital; glad that she'd looked back and seen him phoning someone who every instinct told her had to be Emma; glad that he'd confronted her now in anger, and that she'd hit back. Unforgivably.

Because if he'd stood in the doorway and held out his arms, saying, 'Darling, what is this?' she might indeed have gone to him. And that would have been fatal.

But it wasn't like that. Instead his drawl was icy. 'Hardly wasted, my sweet, when you're throwing me back on the town.'

'Am I supposed to feel some kind of guilt?' She made herself turn, meet his gaze directly. 'I don't think so. If I was the price you had to pay for my father's company, then you've had your money's worth.'

'That's one way of looking at it,' he agreed, the hard mouth twisting. 'But it may not be so easy to step back from this marriage as you think.'

'What are you talking about?'

'Last night,' he said softly, 'when you swept me off my feet, we had unprotected sex, more than once, if memory serves. There could be consequences.'

Darcy's throat tightened. But there couldn't be a baby, she thought desperately. Not when there wasn't a real marriage. Joel didn't need the ties of fatherhood, or to be trapped into staying with her by some sense of duty.

Because that would be more than she could bear.

She found herself saying, almost inaudibly, 'Oh, no, please don't let it be true.'

His voice was harsh. 'My sentiments entirely. It was a stupid, irresponsible way to behave which I swear I never intended. My only excuse is that I wasn't thinking too clearly.' He added sardonically, 'I'm sure I don't have to spell out the reasons.'

Reasons? she thought. What had that mutual explosion of uncontrollable passion and delight to do with any kind of reason?

She said quietly, 'Well, please don't concern yourself too much. If there's a problem there's also, invariably, a solution.' She lifted her chin. 'But from now on, I'm not allowing you anywhere near me. I don't plan to make the same mistake twice. Besides,' she added, 'I have my future career to consider. University, then a real job.' She paused. 'Unless you're planning to break your word over that part of our agreement too.'

'No,' he said, too quietly. 'If that's what you still want, that's what you'll have.'

'Thanks,' she said. 'You have to admit it's an advance on being a sex toy of yours, when you're in the mood. So from now on, all we share is a roof. Do I make myself clear?'

'Oh, yes,' he said. 'You've been very articulate. But you seem to have left human nature out of the equation. You're being very cool, very cerebral about this, Darcy, but what's going to happen when that lovely, eager body of yours won't let you sleep at night? When it tells you that you need me with you, inside you?' His smile grazed her, making her feel as if she'd lost a layer of skin. 'Shall I leave my door ajar, just in case?'

She said thickly, 'You are disgusting.'

'If you say so.' Joel's tone was contemptuous. 'And when I was at my most disgusting, darling, didn't you just love it?'

'You bastard.' Her voice shook. 'Then understand this, too. You do as you wish, but from now on I keep my door locked.'

'Try it,' he told her gently. 'And see what happens.' He allowed her to think about that for a moment, then added, 'By the way, I won't be dining at home tonight, after all. So, please don't bother to wait up for me.'

She sat, staring at the empty doorway. Telling herself that she'd done what she had to. Committed an act of total self-preservation.

And now she had to live with the consequences. One day, one night at a time, until he set her free.

CHAPTER FOURTEEN

DINNER WAS a sombre meal which Mrs Inman served with an almost tangible air of reproach.

When it was over Darcy asked for coffee in the drawing room, and sat for a while pretending to watch television. Trying, she thought, to give the impression that everything was normal, when every scrap of evidence, including the separate bedrooms, indicated the contrary.

I'm fooling no one, she thought wearily. Least of all myself. And I'd be far better off going to bed.

As she closed her bedroom door she glanced at the key, but knew she dared not risk turning it.

She undressed and put on one of her trousseau nightgowns, a frothy chiffon confection that made no attempt at concealment. Then she poured some water into a glass from the carafe on her night table, and took one of the small white capsules she'd brought from Augustina.

She needed to sleep, without thinking or dreaming, in order to deal with whatever tomorrow might bring.

But when, at some time in the long night, Joel's hand touched her shoulder and his voice said her name, she was awake instantly.

He was sitting on the edge of the bed, wearing the crimson robe, and for a moment her throat closed painfully. And then she saw the weariness that shadowed his face in the lamplight, and the infinite sadness in the blue eyes, and she knew.

She sat up, staring at him. Her voice was very quiet. 'It's Daddy, isn't it?'

Joel bent his head. 'They just called from the clinic. There was another crisis. They did all they could, but it was no use. Darcy, I'm so terribly sorry.'

She looked down at the edge of the sheet. Twisted it in her fingers. 'I didn't get the chance to say goodbye. Even though I came all that way…'

A dry sob tore at her throat, then another. And suddenly the tears came too, pouring endlessly down her pale, stricken face.

Joel lay down beside her on the bed, holding her wrapped gently in his arms as she wept. Her cheek was pressed against silk, but the small noises coming from her parted lips were half-stifled by the cool texture of his skin. His hand stroked her hair, her shoulder and arm in quiet, soothing movements. He did not speak.

When at last her helpless grief stilled into long, quivering sobs, Joel got up and went to the bathroom, returning with a damp face cloth to bathe her eyes.

He was blotting away the last of the tears, when there was a knock at the door, and a dressing-gowned Mrs Inman, clearly distressed, came in with a tray of tea. She gave Darcy a look of silent compassion, and disappeared again.

Darcy watched Joel pour the tea. She said, 'I—I don't take sugar.'

'Just this once. It's good for shocks.'

The tea was hot, but there was a core of ice deep inside her that nothing could melt, and she knew with a kind of shame that she was not only mourning for her father, but for the end of her marriage too.

She said, 'Does Aunt Freddie know?'

'Yes,' he said. 'She was there at the clinic when it happened.' He paused. 'Your father had asked her to marry him, once he'd got over the operation.'

'I'm glad,' she said. 'He should have done it a long time ago. They could have had years of happiness together, not this…'

She shook her head. 'We should bring her here. Look after her.'

'Sir Charles was taking her home with him. She's an old friend of his wife's. She'll be fine with them for tonight.'

'He'll want to be buried in Kings Whitnall.'

'Hush,' he said. 'We'll talk about that tomorrow.'

When she'd finished the tea, Joel took the cup and replaced it on the tray. He stood beside the bed, tightening the sash of his robe as he looked down at her. He said, 'Try and get some sleep now.'

'Don't go.' Her voice shook. 'Don't leave me. Please.'

He was silent for a moment, his eyes looking past her, his expression remote, almost weary. Then he said quietly, 'If that's what you want.'

He lay down again beside her, but, as before, on top of the duvet.

She said huskily, 'You'll be cold.'

'I'll survive.' He turned out the lamp, and drew her to him, pillowing her head on his shoulder, and she turned her face into his neck, breathing the essence of him, his unique male scent, letting the warmth of his body be her comfort. And felt his lips brush her hair.

At long last Darcy slept, and never knew the moment when Joel slowly and gently eased himself away from her, getting up from the bed and going silently back to his own room.

The funeral was over, and the last mourners had left the house. So for the first time Darcy was alone, with time to reflect. And to consider the future.

She'd murmured gratitude, shaken hands and offered her cheek to be kissed over and over again during the course of the day, but now a kind of peace was finally descending.

Joel was closeted in the library going through some final paperwork before Gareth Soames, the family solicitor, arrived to read Gavin's will.

Aunt Freddie had gone up to her room to rest, and Darcy had used the same excuse to seek some much-needed privacy, but she'd made no attempt to sleep, even though it had been a rare commodity lately.

Now she stood at her window, a slight figure in her black cashmere dress, looking over the lawns with their light covering of snow, and wondering if she would ever feel warm again.

She could only be thankful that she hadn't been called on to deal with all the legal and financial details that made a loved one's death even harder to bear. That Joel was doing it all, calmly and efficiently.

He'd also been immensely kind, she was forced to admit, particularly to Aunt Freddie, who'd been mutely devastated by her loss. He'd spent hours sitting with her, and talking to her. In fact the older woman had recovered sufficiently to notice that, although he came down to Kings Whitnall each day, he never stayed the night.

'My dear, this isn't right.' Her tone had been concerned. 'You and Joel are only just married. You should be with him far more than this.'

She meant, of course, that they should be sleeping together. That Darcy would learn to cope with the mourning process far better in her husband's arms.

She'd managed to fob Aunt Freddie off with the excuse that Joel had to be in London for early meetings at the company. The Werner Langton board had been thrown into turmoil by Gavin's unexpected death, and the business news pages were saying openly that the knives were out for the new young chairman.

Not that Joel ever gave any sign of the boardroom battles he was fighting. He was invariably cool and controlled during his visits. But then, Darcy reminded herself, he was used to leading a double life.

And she could hardly tell her aunt that the girl Joel loved would soon have her freedom, and he would not be spending his nights alone in London.

Besides, she thought restlessly, Aunt Freddie will discover the truth soon enough, when I set the wheels of our own divorce in motion.

In theory, it was all quite simple. Joel had married her at her father's behest, on the understanding that they would set each other free as soon as it became feasible.

Now, much earlier than anticipated, that moment had come, and the line could finally be drawn under this ill-advised liaison.

After all, there was nothing to keep them together. She didn't even have to rely on Joel financially to launch her on any training course, or new career. And when he left the house later today, there was no real reason why she should ever have to see him again.

Because the terms of her father's will had been explained to her long ago. She was sole heiress to her father's personal fortune, and this house. For the first time in her life, a free and independent woman.

So their divorce would be a mere formality.

And one day, she might even be able to erase the memory of her own voice saying, 'Don't leave me...'

The shame of it still burned inside her like slow fire, she thought. Especially as she had woken to find herself alone once more.

Because she wanted love from Joel, not kindness. Passion, not compassion. Desire, not sympathy.

But he only wanted Emma, so there was nothing left for her except the necessity to part from him. To give him his own freedom to start the new life that was no longer just a dream.

And she had the power to release him. To let him find his happiness.

Besides, she desperately needed him to go. She was far too aware of him physically, instinct telling her each time he entered the house, and making her listen almost painfully for the sound of his footsteps, his voice as he approached any room where she was. And she had to pretend indifference while her heartbeat quickened, and her skin warmed and tingled under the concealment of winter clothing.

Not that he intruded often. He seemed equally keen to avoid further embarrassment by remaining aloof. Yet today she'd sensed his strength like a rock beside her in church, and later standing behind her at the graveside.

Aunt Freddie had clung to his arm, but Darcy had avoided any direct contact with him, walking with her hands at her sides, looking straight ahead.

Accustoming herself, she thought, to being self-sufficient.

She'd been trying to rehearse what to say to Joel. For the sake of her own pride, if nothing else, she should be the one to end the marriage, and she needed to do it well, she thought. Grace under pressure.

There was a quick tap at the door behind her, and Joel came

in. She swung round to face him, arms folded defensively across her body, and saw his brows lift.

'Mr Soames is in the drawing room,' he said. 'I've ordered tea. Are you coming down?'

'Of course,' she said. 'I'll call Aunt Freddie.'

Joel shook his head. 'She's sleeping peacefully. Best not to disturb her.' He held out his hand, but she ignored it, walking past him along the galleried landing and down the stairs.

The tea had already been brought in, and placed on a convenient table. It occurred to Darcy as she handed round the cups and offered the plates of egg mayonnaise and smoked-salmon sandwiches that the sedate and elderly Mr Soames lacked something of his usual composure.

But then, she thought, it was an awkward occasion for everyone.

The niceties over, Mr Soames reached into his briefcase and extracted a document.

He said, 'I understand, Mrs Castille, that your late father kept you apprised in the past of his testamentary intentions.'

'Yes,' she said. 'Always.'

'But you are not, I think, aware that, in view of your marriage, Mr Langton decided to change his will completely.'

'No,' Darcy said. 'He didn't mention it.'

Mr Soames nodded. 'I am sure he would have done so, given time.' He unfolded the document. 'There are still bequests to the staff here and in London, as well as various donations to charity. There is also a considerable lump sum bequeathed to your aunt, but I shall write to her about that.'

He paused. 'The main changes your father requested affect your personal inheritance, Mrs Castille. In the first instance, this house, which you would have inherited outright, has now been left to you jointly with your husband.'

'No,' Darcy whispered. 'No, surely not.'

Mr Soames fiddled with his glasses in obvious embarrassment. 'It is a perfectly usual arrangement, I assure you, Mrs Castille.'

He paused awkwardly. 'The remaining provisions, however, are rather less conventional. The remainder of his personal estate has been used to set up a trust fund for the benefit of any children of your marriage to Mr Castille.'

He coughed delicately. 'I tried to persuade your father that this was rather premature, and it would be better to delay this course of action until you and Mr Castille chose to begin a family, but he was adamant.'

Darcy stared at him, lips parted. She was aware of Joel, motionless beside her as if he'd been carved from granite.

She said hoarsely, 'But he can't do that. He wouldn't...'

'I assure you, Mrs Castille, that your father's instructions were very clear, and the will is perfectly valid.'

'But we won't be having any children.' Her voice broke in desperation. 'In fact, we're getting a divorce just as soon as it can be arranged.'

It was Mr Soames's turn to look shocked. 'If that is the case, Mrs Castille, then the entire remainder of the estate will go to nominated charities instead.' He added quietly, 'Your late father was quite specific about that.'

'Oh, God.' She shook her head. 'This can't be happening. It can't be. There must be something I can do.'

'If so, this isn't the right time or place to talk about it,' Joel said crisply. He got to his feet. 'I'm sorry that you've been burdened with our personal problems in this way, Mr Soames. I presume you'll be writing to us both with copies of the will, and its implications?' He nodded briskly in response to the lawyer's murmured assent. 'Then I'll show you out.'

Darcy remained where she was, seated on the sofa, her hands clenched together in her lap.

Nothing, she thought. I get nothing. Not even this house. My home.

When Joel came back she looked up at him, eyes blazing from her white face. 'Did you know about this?'

'Yes,' he said quietly. 'I thought I'd talked him out of it. In fact, he promised to rethink the whole thing, but he didn't have time.'

He sat down beside her on the wide sofa.

'Darling,' he said gently. 'Darling, listen...'

'Don't call me that.' Her voice rasped. She jumped to her feet, and went over to the window. 'Don't come near me. Don't ever come near me again.'

His mouth hardened. 'Now you're being ridiculous.'

'Am I?' Her laugh cracked in the middle. 'Ridiculous to think I'd be free of you, able to start my own life without being beholden to you in any way?' She shook her head. 'Only you knew differently, didn't you—and you never warned me? But then, why should you? My father ordered you to marry me. Did he also command that you use the honeymoon to get me pregnant? Is that why you forced yourself on me?'

'You don't really think that.' He was on his feet too, his face pale under the tan. 'Darcy, you're terribly upset. You don't know what you're saying.'

'I know I want a divorce,' she said. 'Just as soon as it's legally possible. And that's all either of us need to know.' She drew a quick, harsh breath. 'Separate paths. Separate lives. Beginning now.' She lifted her chin. 'I presume you wouldn't mind if this house was sold? After all, it means nothing to you, and my share would give me independence.'

'But you love this place.'

'Not as much as I love the thought of being free at last. So, will you? Agree to sell, I mean?'

There was a silence, then Joel said quietly, 'If that's what you truly want.'

'Oh, it is,' she said. 'Truly, madly, deeply in fact.' She swallowed. 'So perhaps you'd be good enough to pack your things and leave. I'll expect to hear from your lawyers in due course.'

'That's it? Over?' His voice was incredulous. 'You won't even talk about it?'

She shrugged. 'There's really nothing to discuss. After all, we both have our own plans. So I see no reason why we should meet again, do you?'

'None at all,' he said. 'Except perhaps for this.' He reached her in three strides, and pulled her into his arms, holding her immovable against the hard muscularity of his body. Then his mouth took hers.

It was like no kiss she had ever received in her life before, she realised in some dazed, reeling corner of her mind. Not even when he had led her to the heights of passion had he unleashed such a sensual storm. This was a deliberate, relentless ravishment of her lips, without mercy or tenderness, a punishment rather than a caress, allowing neither protest nor plea. And it was endless.

When at long last he released her she almost staggered backwards, lifting a protective hand to her bruised mouth as she looked up into the cold glitter of his eyes.

'Something to remember me by,' he told her, his voice cool and contemptuous. And then he left.

'I think,' Aunt Freddie said severely, 'that Joel is behaving with amazing generosity, which you do not deserve.'

Darcy took back the letter she'd received that morning from his lawyers. 'I didn't ask him to make over his share of the house to me.' Her tone was defensive.

'No,' her aunt said roundly. 'And he didn't ask to be summarily dumped either after less than a month of marriage. He must be quite desperately hurt. Humiliated, too. How can you treat him like this? Your own husband?'

Darcy bent her head. 'You don't understand,' she said. 'I'm setting Joel free. He can afford to be generous.'

'In view of the absurdly high offer you've had for the house, I'd say he's being prodigal.' Her aunt's tone was tart. 'I presume you're going to accept it?'

Darcy sighed. 'It seems crazy not to,' she said ruefully. 'But I wish it was a private purchaser, instead of some development company I've never heard of.' She sighed again. 'Mr Soames says they'll probably turn the place into luxury flats, and I know how Dad would have hated the idea.'

'Everything changes, my dear,' Aunt Freddie said with quiet sadness. 'And we have to adapt to these changes, however much we dislike them.' She paused. 'Of course, your father would never have envisaged the house coming onto the market. He had this dream of another generation growing up here.'

'Yes,' Darcy said almost inaudibly. 'I know.'

Her aunt gave her a steady look. 'And an astonishing gesture like this calls for some reciprocation, my girl, so I do hope you're

going to thank Joel in person, instead of using some chilly corre-
spondence through third parties. You could at least try and part as
friends, under the circumstances.' She paused. 'Darcy, my dearest, don't let pride or misunderstanding come between you and
happiness, I beg you. Life is too short to leave room for regret.'

Easier said than done, Darcy thought, managing a wan smile.

She'd thought that a life where she didn't have to see Joel or
speak to him might be easier to bear, but she was wrong. It was
just another kind of nightmare. And it didn't stop her thinking
or remembering.

And his decision to forego his share in the sale of the house
had come like a bolt from the blue, placing him once more
squarely in the forefront of her mind. Rekindling all the old
longings, the old pain. Turning her ideas of freedom into a mockery.

Because life without him would be nothing but a cramped and
bitter prison.

She said quietly, 'I'll go round to Chelsea tomorrow, on my
way back to the station.' Then deliberately brightened her tone.
'Now, tell me about this exhibition we're going to see.'

As the taxi entered the square the following morning, she was
already questioning her decision to call there.

I should have come up during the week, she told herself.
Made an appointment to see Joel at Werner Langton. That would
have been more formal, more businesslike.

Well, she thought with an inward sigh. I'm here now. She
paused before leaving the cab to take her wallet from her bag,
and as she did so she saw the front door open and Joel emerge,
followed by a pretty dark-haired girl, moving with the awkward
gait of the heavily pregnant woman. She stayed where she was,
motionless, watching Joel help his companion carefully down
the short flight of steps.

At the bottom she paused, laughing up at him, then took his
hand and placed it on her swollen abdomen as it jutted between
the open edges of her coat. Clearly she wanted him to feel the
baby moving, and Darcy could see the gentleness in his face as
he smiled back at her and made some comment.

The intimacy of the gesture took Darcy by the throat. For a

brief instant she was totally still, swamped by an agony of misery and jealousy that nearly made her moan aloud.

Because Joel would never walk with her like that. Would never gaze at the glorious swell of her body, or feel his child kicking against his hand. Because she knew for certain now that she wasn't pregnant, and the awareness of that made her feel sick with despair and loneliness.

But that was soon followed by the worse fear that Joel would glance across the road and see her there. Watching them together. And the humiliation of that would crucify her.

'You getting out, love, or what?' The driver craned his neck to look at her.

'I've changed my mind,' she said, and her voice was almost calm. 'Will you take me to Victoria Station instead, please?'

It seemed strange to think she would not be spending another Christmas at Kings Whitnall, Darcy thought, watching the flames leaping in the hearth. She would not sit in front of many more fires there either.

Contracts had been exchanged with almost frightening speed, and the purchase would be completed by the end of the week. But by that time she would be staying in London at her aunt's flat, while they began preparations for Christmas, and she decided what to do with her future.

Her things were already packed, and waiting. The company who'd bought the house had expressed an interest in the furniture, too. She'd chosen the things—her father's desk, and the grand piano among others—that she wanted to store for her own home when she found it. All she had to do now was wait for some suit from the buyers to come and pass judgement on the rest. Otherwise it would all go to auction.

As she heard the door bell peal, she rose, straightening her shoulders. One more unpleasant task, she thought, and then it would be all over. She could maybe start looking forward, instead of back. Indeed, she would have to, although she still had no clear idea how her future life would take shape.

When the drawing-room door opened she looked up with a cool, formal smile, then tensed as Joel walked into the room, spots of rain gleaming on the shoulders of his dark blue overcoat.

For a moment, Darcy thought she must be hallucinating. When she spoke her voice was a croak. 'What are you doing here?'

'I've come to talk about furniture,' he said. 'For a house I've just bought.'

'You bought?' She felt dazed. 'But that's not possible. The purchasers are a development company I've never heard of.'

'My father's company,' he said. 'He was into construction and property development, and he ended up a millionaire, several times over. The man who was his second in command has been running it for me in France, but he wants to retire soon, so I shall have to take the reins myself before too long. But I shall still keep a foothold in England.'

She went on staring at him. Her lips moved but no sound emerged. At last, she managed, 'Not this house, please. Not this.'

'Why not?' He halted where he was, unfastening his coat and shrugging it off. It occurred to her that he looked thinner. Wearier.

'Because it was my home, and I loved it.' There were tears thick in her throat, and hurting at the backs of her eyes. *And I can't bear to think of you living here with Emma, and the baby. Loving someone else here. Having children of your own.*

She shook her head. 'I can't believe you could be so cruel. Do I really deserve this?'

'God knows what either of us deserve,' Joel said shortly. 'But the house is mine, and the money will hit your account on Friday. You can use it to make all your plans and dreams come true, or you can take it to Monte Carlo and lose the lot on the roulette wheel. That's not important.'

His voice deepened into intensity. 'But what you have to know is that, divorced or married, this is still your home, and it will always be here waiting for you.' She saw him swallow. 'As I will,' he added harshly. 'If this precious freedom of yours ever palls.'

She turned away, her voice husky, 'Please, you mustn't say things like that. It's wrong.'

'Yes,' he said with bitterness. 'Wrong from the start, and downhill all the way since then.' He shook his head. 'When I asked you to marry me, I knew you didn't love me, Darcy, not in the way I wanted. But I thought I could make you fall in love with me a little—or, at least, in lust. I told myself that if our bodies were close, then our hearts and minds must follow.

'But I soon discovered that wasn't true. That no matter what happened between us at night, you couldn't wait to be rid of me when daylight came.'

He paused. 'When we came back to London, and you insisted on your own room, I began to wonder just how much rejection I could take.'

Darcy swung back to face him. 'You can say that? And just where does your cousin Emma feature in all this?' Her own tone was equally harsh. 'Are you planning some kind of *ménage à trois*? Or are you going to leave her in Chelsea, and visit me at weekends?'

'Emma,' Joel repeated as if he'd never heard the name before. 'What the hell has she to do with anything?'

'Everything, I'd say. After all, she's left her husband for you.' She added with difficulty, 'And she's been living with you in London.'

'Emma,' he said, grimly, 'is now at home in the country with her parents, whom I had to trace all round the damned Australian outback. I can't tell you how long it took.

'They'd asked me to look after her while they were away, because they were worried about the state of her marriage. I had to agree, because they're family, and they were damned good to me when I was a boy, but frankly I'd rather have stuck my head into a nest of killer bees.'

Darcy was beginning to tremble inside. She said, 'I don't understand. You *love* Emma.'

He said quietly, 'Emma was the younger sister I never had. She has many good qualities, but she's always been spoiled rotten, and there were times when I could cheerfully have shaken her until she rattled.' He shook his head. 'This past couple of months being a case in point.'

He sat down on the sofa. 'I seem to have spent a lot of my

life heading her off from unsuitable men, but the Harry Metcalfe thing began when I was out of the country, and she persuaded her parents that this time it was real love.

'She discovered she was pregnant when she'd also just found out that Harry had been playing away at a serious level. They tried to patch things up, but it didn't work, and the wheels came off for the last time just around the time of our wedding.

'Because she knew her parents had asked me to watch out for her, Em naturally decided this meant I was at her total beck and call. The fact that I was on my honeymoon didn't seem to occur to her.' He added dispassionately, 'She's sweet, but totally self-centred. I just hope that the baby's arrival may change her focus.'

'But she was with you in Chelsea,' Darcy protested. 'I saw you together,' she added unguardedly.

He frowned. 'What were you doing there?'

'I—I wanted to thank you—about the house.'

'But you didn't,' he said. 'You never came near. You wrote me a very cold note instead.'

She bent her head. 'I didn't want to impinge.'

'If you'd rung the bell,' he said slowly, 'you'd have met my aunt and uncle. They were staying there too.' The corners of his mouth twisted into a reluctant grin. 'It was hell on wheels. Recriminations from morning to night, and Em convinced she was about to go into premature labour brought on by stress. Every time the baby moved, we all had to know about it.'

He looked at her. 'But I could think of nothing but you, Darcy, and what a bloody mess I'd made of our lives. The love we weren't going to share. The children we would never have.

'Which is why I decided to buy this house, to pay for the independence you seemed to prize above everything else. Certainly above anything we might have together.

'I knew, of course, you wouldn't take the money from me if I simply offered it to you. You've never wanted anything from me.

'You wouldn't even wear the caftan I bought you on Augustina,' he added with a touch of bitterness. 'Even though you'd have looked incredibly beautiful in it. Instead, you insisted on muffling yourself in that towelling effort. It was only a little thing, but it made me feel utterly defeated.'

'My God.' Darcy stared at him open-mouthed. 'You mean, it was a present from *you*?'

'Who else could it have been from?'

She swallowed. 'I thought it was Drew Maidstone, winding you up.'

'Ah,' he said. 'So what happened to it?'

She didn't dare look at him. 'I threw it away.'

'Really?' He was thoughtful for a moment. 'Then let's hope it was found by a dustman with taste.'

'You have every right to be angry…'

'Where you're concerned,' he said gently, 'I have no rights at all. But if you wanted to make amends for the caftan, you could come and sit beside me. There's something I need to ask you.'

She complied, putting a discreet distance between them, her hands folded in her lap, and looking anywhere but at him.

'Darcy,' he said quietly, 'will you have dinner with me one night? And may I send you flowers that my secretary hasn't chosen?'

She said in a small voice, 'Joel, you have the company. You're going to win your battles with the board, so you don't have to pretend any more, or stick to the deal my father pushed you into.'

'Is that what you think?' He possessed himself of her two tense fists, uncurling them and stroking her fingers softly. 'Darcy, it was seeing your photograph and discovering you were Gavin's daughter that made me agree to take on Werner Langton in the first place. Nothing else.'

He was silent for a moment, then he said with difficulty, 'Darcy, when I walked into that room at the club two years ago and saw you, the world stopped. I thought to myself, so here she is at last. The one girl.

'And then I realised what you were, and why you were there, and I felt sick to my stomach, crucified, because life had just played me the dirtiest of all possible tricks.'

He looked at her, his eyes haunted. 'I nearly came after you that night. I shall always regret that I didn't. That I listened to that contemptible bastard, or gave his lies a moment's credence.

'But I couldn't get you out of my mind, no matter how hard I tried. Then, when I saw you again, met you, I was lost again. Of course, I told myself at first that I was simply intrigued. That I wanted to find out what made you tick. But I was fooling myself.

'And it wasn't your father's idea that we should marry. It was all my doing. As I told him, for me it was love at first sight.'

'But you said you cared for someone who was involved elsewhere,' she whispered. 'I knew it was Emma. It couldn't be anyone else.'

'My love, it was you. And you're the only reason I'm still around. Still fighting my corner at Werner Langton. Because I've been hoping against hope that one day, however far in the future, you might want to be my wife in every sense of the word. My companion, my lover, and the joy of my heart.'

His voice was suddenly husky. 'I came down here today because I couldn't stay away any longer. I could, rather I should have sent someone else, but I needed to see you so badly. To hear your voice. Smell your perfume in the air. Maybe touch your hand. I thought, even if she sends me away again, I'll have that at least.'

She looked down at the lean brown fingers clasping hers, then bent her head and kissed them swiftly and sweetly. 'You thought that?' Her voice broke. 'Joel, I don't want to send you away. I never did. But, you see, everyone told me from the first that it was Emma you really wanted. And I couldn't bear to be second best, not when I loved you so.'

'My darling idiot.' His voice was immensely tender. 'Don't you know that there'll never be anyone else in my life but you? You gave me a dream, Darcy. The only one I'll ever need.'

He looked down at her bare hands. 'What happened to my rings? Another garbage truck?'

'No, they're up in my bedroom.' She paused, looking at him under her lashes. 'I thought perhaps you might help me look for them.'

Joel framed her face in his hands. He kissed her forehead, her eyes and, gently, her parted lips.

'I think,' he said, steadying his breathing with an effort, 'that it could be a very long search. But there is one condition.'

'Which is?' The warmth of desire was making her breathless.

'That when I wake up tomorrow morning, you'll still be in my arms.' His voice was almost fierce. 'Man and wife, Darcy. I'll settle for nothing less.'

She moved closer, pressing her lips to his throat, feeling his pulse leap.

'Man and wife,' she whispered, softly, pleasurably. 'It's a deal.'

HARLEQUIN®
Presents

The world's bestselling romance series...
The series that brings you your favorite authors,
month after month:

Helen Bianchin...Emma Darcy
Lynne Graham...Penny Jordan
Miranda Lee...Sandra Marton
Anne Mather...Carole Mortimer
Susan Napier...Michelle Reid

and many more uniquely talented authors!

Wealthy, powerful, gorgeous men...
Women who have feelings just like your own...
The stories you love, set in exotic, glamorous locations...

HARLEQUIN®
Presents

Seduction and Passion Guaranteed!

HPDIR104

HARLEQUIN *Presents*®

Bedded by... *Blackmail*

Forced to bed...then to wed?

BOUGHT BY HER HUSBAND
by Sharon Kendrick

For Max Quintano, blackmailing
Sophie into becoming his mistress
was simple—she'd do anything to
protect her family. Now she's
beholden to him, until she
discovers why he hates her....

Dare to read it?

On sale July 2006

HARLEQUIN *Presents*

Coming Next Month

#2547 PRINCE OF THE DESERT Penny Jordan
Arabian Nights

Gwynneth had vowed that she would never become a slave to passion. But one hot night of lovemaking with a stranger from the desert has left her fevered and unsure. Little does Gwynneth know that she shared a bed with Sheikh Tariq bin Salud.

#2548 THE SCORSOLINI MARRIAGE BARGAIN Lucy Monroe
Royal Brides

Claudio Scorsolini married Therese for convenience only. So when Therese starts to fall in love with her husband, she tries to end the marriage—for both their sakes. But Claudio isn't ready to let her go.

#2549 NAKED IN HIS ARMS Sandra Marton
UnCut

When ex-Special Forces agent Alexander Knight is called upon to protect the beautiful Cara Prescott, his only choice is to hide her on his private island. But can Alex keep Cara from harm when he has no idea how dangerous the truth really is?

#2550 THE SECRET BABY REVENGE Emma Darcy
Latin Lovers

Joaquin Luis Sola is proud and passionate and yearns to possess beautiful Nicole Ashton. Nicole reluctantly offers herself to him, if he will pay her debts. This proposition promises that Quin will see a most satisfying return.

#2551 AT THE GREEK TYCOON'S BIDDING Cathy Williams
Greek Tycoons

Heather is different from Greek businessman Theo Miquel's usual prey: frumpy, far too talkative and his office cleaner. But Theo could see she would be perfect for an affair—at his beck and call until he tires of her. But Heather won't stay at her boss's bidding!

#2552 THE ITALIAN'S CONVENIENT WIFE Catherine Spencer
Italian Husbands

When Paolo Rainero's niece and nephew are orphaned, his solution is to marry Caroline Leighton, their American aunt, with whom Paolo once had a fling. Their desire is rekindled from years before—but Caroline has a secret....

#2553 THE JET-SET SEDUCTION Sandra Field
Foreign Affairs

From the moment Slade Carruthers lays eyes on Clea Chardin he knows he must have her. But Clea has a reputation, and Slade isn't a man to share his spoils. If Clea wants to come to his bed, she will come on his terms.

#2554 MISTRESS ON DEMAND Maggie Cox
Mistress to a Millionaire

Rich and irresistible, property tycoon Dominic van Straten lived in an entirely different world from Sophie's. But after their reckless hot encounter, Dominic wanted her available whenever he needed her.

HPCNM0606